"What would be your feelings towards an illegitimate child?"

Frederica gasped and sprang to her feet. "It is the outside of enough that you wish to hire a...a fancy woman in the first place, my lord. But that you would actually *plan* for children to result from such a union..." She headed for the library door. "I believe I've heard quite enough, Lord Seabrooke," she said scathingly over her shoulder.

With two long strides, Lord Seabrooke placed himself between her and the door. "Miss Cherrystone, I'm not sure what bee you have in your bonnet, but I beg you to sit down and hear me out. I'll not have you leaving in this state of mind, to spread scandal about the streets of London when I have been at such pains to keep this quiet."

Frederica was so angry she was near tears. How dare he betroth himself to her and then advertise openly for a mistress!

Regency England: 1811-1820

*"It was the best of times,
it was the worst of times...."*

As George III languished in madness, the
pampered and profligate Prince of Wales led the
land in revelry and the elegant Beau Brummel set
the style. Across the Channel, Napoleon continued
to plot against the English until his final exile to
St. Helena. Across the Atlantic, America renewed
hostilities with an old adversary, declaring war on
Britain in 1812. At home, Society glittered, love
matches abounded and poets such as Lord Byron
flourished. It was a time of heroes and villains, a
time of unrelenting charm and gaiety, when entire
fortunes were won or lost on a turn of the dice and
reputation was all. A dazzling period that left its
mark on two continents and whose very name
became a byword for elegance and romance.

Books by Brenda Hiatt

HARLEQUIN REGENCY ROMANCE

70—GABRIELLA
81—THE UGLY DUCKLING
91—LORD DEARBORN'S DESTINY

Don't miss any of our special offers. Write to us at the
following address for information on our newest releases.

Harlequin Reader Service
P.O. Box 1397, Buffalo, NY 14240
Canadian address: P.O. Box 603,
Fort Erie, Ont. L2A 5X3

DARING DECEPTION
Brenda Hiatt

Harlequin Books

TORONTO • NEW YORK • LONDON
AMSTERDAM • PARIS • SYDNEY • HAMBURG
STOCKHOLM • ATHENS • TOKYO • MILAN
MADRID • WARSAW • BUDAPEST • AUCKLAND

In memory of my father, Howard H. Hiatt

Published July 1993

ISBN 0-373-31202-4

DARING DECEPTION

CHAPTER ONE

GAVIN ALEXANDER, lately 6th Earl of Seabrooke, observed the growing dismay on the face of the young man before him and sighed. He should have known his own incredible luck over the past few hours was too good to be true, and so it apparently was. The lad couldn't pay up.

"I'll accept your vowels, of course, Chesterton," Lord Seabrooke said brusquely. Frustrated as he was, it was not in him to humiliate the boy publicly. "You may redeem them later in the week."

Sir Thomas chewed his lower lip, glancing quickly about at the interested spectators who had gathered to watch the final stages of the evening's deepest game, before meeting his opponent's eye. "Might I have a word with you privately, sir?" he asked in a shaky undertone.

Seabrooke inclined his head, masking fierce disappointment with the lightly amused nonchalance that came so easily now after years of practice. "You've all had your entertainment," he said to their audience. "Our terms of payment can be of no interest to you whatever." Though there was nothing overtly threatening in either words or tone, the crowd of gentlemen melted away at once.

"I—I seem to have a problem," stammered the young baronet as soon as they were alone. He raked agitated fingers through his thick shock of fair hair as he stared despondently down at the table, unable to meet the other man's eyes.

"You don't have the means to pay your gaming debts. Yes, I had gathered that." Seabrooke's voice was cold now. He had needed those winnings so desperately! "You realize that I could have you barred from White's for playing under false pretences."

Sir Thomas's head came up at once. "It was no such thing!" he declared hotly. "The Chesterton fortune is every bit as extensive as I said. I just don't exactly... have access to it at the moment. It is tied up in trust, you see."

A flame of renewed hope sprang up in Gavin's breast. "But the money is yours?"

"Yes, yes, of course! Well, mine and my sister's, anyway. The terms of m' father's will were rather... irregular." Lord Seabrooke thought he detected a certain bitterness in the lad's voice. "My share will more than cover your twelve thousand pounds, but my allowance won't make a dent in it. In fact, my pockets are practically to let till next quarter." The despair was back in his eyes, and Seabrooke felt his brief hope wither.

His circumstances were becoming increasingly desperate.

Despite his lack of a title, Major Gavin Alexander had cut quite a dash in fashionable London, especially with the ladies. The slight limp his war injury had left him seemed to make him an even more romantic figure in their eyes. His leisure hours had been spent in amusements reputable and disreputable, and his near-notoriety gained him entry into places few noblemen frequented. This latter had made him particularly useful to the wartime government, though he could no longer serve in combat.

Never precisely wealthy, he had managed to live well enough on what the War Office paid him—until recently.

When the news reached him that his Uncle Edmund, a virtual stranger due to a longstanding feud between the 5th earl and Gavin's late father, had succumbed to a fever, the new Lord Seabrooke had been both stunned and elated. Giving notice at Whitehall, he had at once travelled north to his new holdings, where another shock awaited him: instead of the tidy fortune he had been led to expect, his uncle had left him a mountain of debt. Gavin sold off the unentailed lands to pay the mortgages, and depleted his own savings, but still there were bills unpaid.

Never one to repine, he had eventually returned to Town and lived much as he ever had. Turning out the tenants to take up residence in Seabrooke House, he managed to keep up a pretence of wealth so as not to be denied admittance to the better clubs, where his chief hope of salvation lay. He did have one other: as Lord Seabrooke, he found himself in even greater demand by the Town's hostesses—and their daughters.

After the skirmishes of the spring, Napoleon had finally, irrevocably, been defeated, effectively eliminating Gavin's position with the War Office. Already his credit was beginning to run out; soon the mamas of certain heiresses would get wind of it and warn their daughters away from him. And now he found himself saddled with a new responsibility, one that honour would not allow him to shirk and that made the recoupment of his finances absolutely essential.

When the young buck before him had come into White's looking for a game, boasting of his broad estates and vast fortune, Seabrooke was not the only one who saw him as a wonderfully plump pigeon, ripe to be plucked. While the others had been mainly amused by the young man's airs, however, Seabrooke had perceived in him the miracle he so desperately needed. Now it appeared that he had given thanks prematurely.

"And when, precisely, will you have control of your portion of the trust?" he asked with more resignation than hope.

"Not till I turn five and twenty," replied Sir Thomas dolefully, poking at the cards before him with one forefinger. "Nearly four years. Frederica gets hers when she marries, but at the rate she's going that may well be even longer. Surely there must be some way to break this damned trust. A debt of honour, after all…"

"Your sister is unmarried?" asked Lord Seabrooke casually, seized by a sudden inspiration born of dire necessity. "Tell me about her."

MISS FREDERICA CHESTERTON was having an extremely trying day. She had been wakened before dawn by the shrieking of a housemaid, only to discover that the silly girl's hysterics were precipitated by nothing more than the sight of one of Frederica's pet mice. The maid was new, and had not yet grown accustomed to her mistress's unusual menagerie.

On coming downstairs, Frederica had found that someone had neglected to latch the scullery door, and one of the Angora goats had come into the kitchen. Cook was furious and threatening to give notice, and by the time Frederica had soothed him, her peacock,

Fanfare, was screaming loudly for his breakfast. An hour later, the steward appeared to inform her that the late-summer rains had ruined the barley crop.

Mrs. Gresham, the aging housekeeper, was in a sour mood after being wakened by the peacock and aroused Cook's ire in turn by suggesting the porridge was lumpy. Frederica managed to smooth things over between the habitual combatants, pacifying Mrs. Gresham with one of Cook's puff pastries in place of the reviled porridge. Then the accounts had to be gone over, and Frederica found that she had made an error last month that necessitated refiguring two complete columns.

After ruining three pen nibs, hunting down the housekeeper's missing keys and separating two young kitchen maids who were pelting each other with flour, Frederica finally retreated to the little back parlour with a tea tray, determined to have an hour to herself to recover her spirits and energy. She had taken only one sip, however, when yet another interruption occurred.

"Good afternoon, Freddie." A familiar figure appeared without warning in the doorway. Though the young man standing there possessed blond hair, while Frederica's curls were the colour of brightly polished copper, there was a similarity between the two that marked them at once as brother and sister.

"Thomas! I thought you still in London." Frederica rose with a welcoming smile. One look at her brother's handsome countenance, however, told her that he was highly agitated about something. "Is anything wrong?" After everything else that had happened today, it seemed all too likely.

Despite the fact that she was a year younger, Frederica had tended to mother Thomas ever since their own mother's death nearly ten years before. In vain she reminded herself that he was one and twenty now, a man grown. Of late he had begun to resent her ordering of their lives, she knew. In fact, when he had left for Town a few weeks before, she had feared that he might do something foolish merely to prove his independence.

"You haven't gotten into some sort of trouble, have you, dear?" she asked with ready concern. Looking at him now, she could not help seeing the scapegrace lad he had been, to be soothed, shielded and advised, as always.

Thomas, however, immediately donned a charming smile and came forward to embrace her. "Wrong? Of course not, Freddie. Quite the opposite, in fact. I've come to offer you my heartiest congratulations."

Frederica stiffened in her brother's clasp, drawing back to regard him warily. "Congratulations? Congratulations for what, Thomas?"

"Why, on your betrothal to the Earl of Seabrooke. Quite a respectable match, considering you've not been to Town, eh? Imagine, my little sister a countess!"

"Have you taken leave of your senses?" she demanded, pulling free of him. "How can I possibly be betrothed to a man I have never met?" Examining Thomas through narrowed eyes, she wondered whether he might be foxed, early in the day though it was.

"No, Frederica, I have finally come to my senses," declared Thomas stoutly, though he refused to meet his sister's gaze. "I have come to realize that I've been shirking many of my responsibilities—to the estate and especially, to you."

Frederica stared at her brother open-mouthed. She had never seen him in this mood before and found herself, uncharacteristically, at a loss for words.

"I'm a man now, and it is time I had a care for your future," Thomas went on, in what was beginning to sound suspiciously like a rehearsed speech. "You cannot spend your life running my household, you know. You are far too capable—and pretty—to settle for that. No, it is time you had a household of your own, one worthy of your merit.

"I shall require you to go over the accounts with me, so that I may familiarize myself with the workings of the estate. Then I'll have a conference with our steward—what's his name?" He faltered briefly, looking to her for assistance.

"Bridges," replied Frederica dazedly, undecided whether to be outraged or amused at Thomas's sudden decision to grow up.

"Bridges. Of course." He clasped his hands behind his back and began to pace the room. "He can continue to oversee all the day-to-day details, but he will now answer to me instead of you. I can't imagine what Father was thinking of to suggest that you manage the estate in the first place. It's hardly fitting for a woman."

Frederica knew very well what their father had been thinking when he stipulated in his will that she have the handling of Maple Hill and the surrounding estate. During the five years before his death, from the time she was barely in her teens, it had been Frederica rather than Thomas who had taken a keen interest in all that went into running a large household and its adjacent farms. She had set herself to learn every aspect of management, from consulting with Cook to visiting the

tenant families, and had gradually taken on all the responsibilities that would have been her mother's, had
she lived, as well as many of her father's. Thomas,
meanwhile, had eluded all his parent's efforts to edu-
cate him as befitted an heir, often spending even his
holidays at Eton, and then Oxford, with his friends.

"It is all very well you are finally taking an interest
in Maple Hill," Frederica said, finding her tongue at
last. "But what has that to do with my marrying? I
cannot believe you would make such a decision for my
future without consulting me. Come, tell me this is one
of your hoaxes, Thomas."

"No, Freddie, it is not. I am persuaded that Seabrooke will make you a splendid husband. You will
doubtless thank me when you grow accustomed to the
idea." His tone was lofty, but he still avoided her eye.

Frederica's slow temper finally reached its boiling
point. "*Thank* you? For flippantly arranging the rest
of my life without so much as a by-your-leave? I think
not! I would never have encouraged you to go to London had I known you would do something so shatter-
brained. Now I suppose it will be up to me to write to
this Lord Seabrooke to cry off, as if I had nothing better with which to occupy my time."

"It is too late for that," Thomas informed her
bluntly. "The contracts have already been drawn up.
To cry off now would cause no end of scandal and be
exceedingly awkward for all concerned."

He had no intention of telling her just how awkward. In payment of his gaming debt, he had settled
twelve thousand pounds of Frederica's inheritance on
Lord Seabrooke in advance. If the betrothal were cancelled, he would still owe the man that impossible sum.
During the journey home, Sir Thomas had managed to

convince himself that he truly was acting in his sister's best interests, never realizing that Lord Seabrooke himself had done much to plant that satisfactory idea in his head.

Frederica took three deep breaths, as her old governess had always recommended she do in times of stress. It was being borne in upon her that her brother actually wished her to honour this outrageous commitment. Biting back another angry retort, she determined to discover all the particulars involved. Organized to a fault, Frederica preferred to have all the facts at her disposal before dealing with any problem. The approach had served her well in the past, and she saw no reason to deviate from it now.

"I don't recall that I've heard you mention Lord Seabrooke before, Thomas," she said with what she felt was laudable calm. "Is he someone you met at Oxford?"

"No, I met him for the first time during my visit to London. I'm sure you will like him, Freddie. He's a capital fellow. Fought on the Peninsula against Boney."

Frederica was aghast. "You just met him? Thomas, for all you know he might be no more than a fortune-hunter!"

For the first time, Thomas looked uncomfortable. "Shouldn't think so," he said, frowning. "He's a member at all the clubs, even White's. It's deuced hard to get in there. I should know—I had to have two friends put in a word for me to be admitted. They'd never allow a fortune-hunter in." He spoke more confidently now.

"Not if he announced the fact," Frederica returned acidly. She had not missed Thomas's discomfort and pressed harder. "So you know virtually nothing about the man, for all your fine speeches, other than his title and service record."

"It's not as though I'm forcing you to wed some toothless old roué, after all," said Thomas defensively. "Seabrooke is well enough looking and can't be much past thirty—came into his title just a few months ago, I believe. He's a bang-up Corinthian and vastly in demand. Most girls would jump at the chance to marry him."

"I am not 'most girls,' Thomas. I'd prefer to know a bit more about a man before tying myself to him for life. Your precious Lord Seabrooke could be a murderer or a highwayman for all you know of him. But I suppose I must wait to discover such things until after I am his wife." Frederica made no effort to conceal her bitterness, hoping that it would help to dissuade her brother from his mad scheme.

"Now, Freddie, you know I'd never expect you to marry a scoundrel," said Thomas soothingly, patting her hand in a manner Frederica found maddeningly condescending. "Seabrooke is quite the gentleman. You must trust me."

She thought rapidly. "You are certain you would not force me to marry a scoundrel, Thomas?" she asked carefully.

"Of course not! You're my sister, after all." His tone was indignant.

"So if it were to transpire that your Lord Seabrooke *is* a scoundrel, you would allow me to cry off?"

Thomas paused at that, but then shrugged. "Yes. But he is no scoundrel, I assure you. Oh, he has a bit of a reputation as a rake, I'll grant you that—what red-blooded blade don't? Nothing you need worry about, though."

Frederica was smiling grimly now. "I'll be the judge of that, Thomas. I plan to do a bit of investigating about the Earl of Seabrooke. If I can prove that he's got more than a 'bit of a reputation,' that he's a fortune-hunter or in any way dishonourable, I'll expect you to hold to your promise."

Thomas was taken aback, but only for a moment. After all, what could she possibly discover that he would not have heard about in Town? He *had* asked his friends about the man before having the papers drawn up—he wasn't a complete nodcock! Doubtless Frederica simply meant to write a few letters. And even if she went to London herself, which he thought unlikely in the extreme, he was confident that there was nothing really wrong with Seabrooke. He'd stake his own reputation on that, even after such a short acquaintance.

And if there were something—something that actually merited the label of "scoundrel"—well, he'd just have to find another way to raise twelve thousand pounds. He owed his sister too much to do otherwise.

Thomas looked at her with affection, realizing for the first time what a prize she might be considered, with her cascading copper curls, wide green eyes and flawless complexion—and a fortune, to boot.

"Very well, Freddie," he finally said, "investigate away. You'll see Seabrooke is a right 'un. And then I'll expect you to do your part. I'm sure you have no more desire to end up an ape leader—er, a spinster—than I have to see you one. You are twenty already and you still resist making your come-out in Town. I can't imagine how you ever expect to catch a husband holed up here at Maple Hill. Why, you don't even go to the local assemblies since Father died."

"I'd rather remain unwed to my dying day than be bound to a man I can't love or respect," his sister retorted, her eyes glinting. "And despite what you say, Thomas, no man who would betroth himself to a lady sight unseen can be all that he should be. If he were as sought after as you say, why should he do so? I'll discover something to his discredit, never fear! And I shall hold you to your promise when I do." Her face set, Frederica strode from the room.

Sir Thomas watched her go, a slight frown creasing his handsome brow. All in all, the interview had gone better than he had expected. At least she had not refused outright, as he had feared. If she had, he doubted he could have forced her to the match. Still, he could not recall Frederica ever failing at a task she set her mind to, and she had looked uncommonly determined this time. Could he possibly have misjudged Lord Seabrooke?

His brow cleared and he shrugged. If he had, no doubt Frederica would discover it for him. He had decided years ago that there was never any point in worrying about things one could not change, particularly if they were unpleasant. Accordingly, Sir Thomas put the entire matter from his mind and sat down to consume the remainder of Frederica's tea and cakes.

CHAPTER TWO

FREDERICA WENT STRAIGHT to the study to pull pen and paper from her desk. She knew Thomas had only made that promise because he thought she could have no way of finding out anything of substance about his precious Lord Seabrooke, but she had a secret weapon that he had doubtless overlooked—her old governess, Miss Milliken.

In the more than ten years Frederica had known her, Miss Milliken had gradually moved from the position of governess to that of friend and confidante. She and Frederica had enjoyed an unusually close relationship based on a similarity of tastes and a sincere affection for each other, and it was only upon the death of Miss Milliken's mother a year ago that the woman had left Maple Hill to keep house for her father on the outskirts of London.

It was to Miss Milliken that Frederica owed a large part of her purposeful, organized approach to life's setbacks and challenges. A lifelong student of ancient military campaigns, Miss Milliken believed strongly that a carefully planned strategy could overcome any problem, from knotted embroidery thread to a fire in the stables. In addition, Frederica had discovered over the years that her governess was possessed of a vast network of friends and acquaintances in Town and elsewhere, whose varying experiences and expertise were occasionally sought, through letters, to clarify some point in her charge's education. Frederica suspected that if anyone could assist her in her present quest, Miss Milliken could. Quickly, she penned her letter.

TO FREDERICA'S SURPRISE, Thomas really did seem intent during the next few days on learning the workings of the estate. Instead of growing bored and changing the subject as he had whenever their father had attempted to instruct him, he asked numerous questions and demanded to be taken over every farm and holding. Frederica, having no idea how far guilt and the bad scare he had received in London had motivated the sudden change, supposed that he must finally be growing up.

"Here is the school I've been telling you about," she said as they approached the long, low building at one end of the village, on yet another tour during his first week at home. "I'm really very proud of it. In the two years since I opened it, nearly a dozen girls have learned to read, write and sew, substantially broadening their prospects. One has even obtained a position as a shop-girl in Broadgate."

"You teach them yourself?" asked Thomas in amazement.

"No, I've managed to find a schoolmistress, though I did so at the outset. I still try to spend some time here every week, teaching drawing to a few of the more talented girls and helping out with some of the youngest ones. Two of the older girls have started a nursery of sorts to allow their mothers a respite at home."

They entered the rear of the building as she spoke, and several children ranging in age from two to six ran forward to greet her with hugs and kisses.

"Good morning, Sarah! How are you today, Mary? Jane, is your cold better?" She greeted each child warmly while Sir Thomas looked on in bemusement. Rising after a moment, she spoke briefly to one of the young women in charge of the youngsters before opening a door to the main room of the schoolhouse.

"We won't go in to disturb the lessons, but I wanted you to have a peek," she said in an undertone to her brother. Looking over her shoulder, he saw a dozen or more girls seated at small wooden desks, listening attentively to a matronly, bespectacled woman at the front of the room. Closing the door again, she turned to him. "I feel this school has truly made a difference in the lives of these girls and their families. It's been extremely rewarding." Her look challenged him.

Thomas led her back outdoors before replying. "I had no idea, Freddie," he said, shaking his head. "But I promise to keep the school running if...when...well, you know."

Frederica gave him a lopsided discerning smile. "That's very comforting, to be sure, but I fully intend to see to it myself." It was the closest they had come to discussing her betrothal since that first conversation. "I've not forgotten your promise, Thomas."

"Yes, well, I have been rethinking the matter, Freddie," he said slowly.

"Yes?" She felt a surge of triumph. He was going to call it off!

"I think you should come to Town with me for the Little Season at the end of September. Meet Seabrooke yourself. Who knows, you may discover you like him well enough after all.''

Frederica glared at him. "So that he may turn on his charm to bamboozle me as he evidently has you? No, thank you. The face he'll show me as his wife will doubtless be quite different from the one he puts on for Society. Meeting him at a ball or a musicale will prove nothing.''

Thomas let out a gusty sigh. "It was just a thought. Have it your own way, then—but I warn you, Freddie, you cannot take forever to prove your silly theory. Seabrooke and I discussed a Christmas wedding.''

"Christmas? *This* Christmas? Thomas, you did not mention that!'' Frederica was appalled. "That's scarcely four months away!''

"Well, if he's the blackguard you think, no doubt you can discover it in half that time,'' said Thomas, nettled. How was it that Freddie could always make him feel so guilty? "Now, weren't you going to show me the drainage ditches?''

To Frederica's vast relief there was a letter awaiting her from Miss Milliken upon her return to the house an hour later. She tore it open eagerly, scanned its brief contents and went at once in search of her brother.

"Thomas,'' she said when she found him in the stables looking over the carriage horses, "I've just had a letter from Miss Milliken. You know, my old governess,'' she reminded him when he looked blank. "She has asked me to visit her, and I mean to go. I believe I shall find her a soothing influence—something I stand in need of just now.'' She kept her eyes wide and guileless, assuming a long-suffering look.

"That sounds a capital idea, Freddie,'' her brother replied cheerfully. "If I remember her rightly, she'll be just the one to talk some sense into you. Didn't she go to her father in the country somewhere?"

"Yes," said Frederica, not feeling it necessary to disclose the precise location of the house. "I thought I would leave on the morrow. 'Tis less than half a day's drive."

"I'll be up to see you off. Write to me if you change your mind about the Little Season so that I may make preparations."

"Of course I shall." Frederica turned back to the house to make the necessary arrangements for her first-ever prolonged absence from Maple Hill, telling herself that it would do Thomas good to have the running of it to himself for a bit. Humming a stirring march under her breath, she thought over what she hoped to accomplish. Never inform the enemy of your intentions, that was what Miss Milliken had always said.

BEFORE TEATIME the next day Frederica's carriage drew up in front of the Millikens' small, neat cottage. As she was giving the manservant directions about her trunks and caged pets—mice and peacock only, for the goats would have been most impractical to transport—her old friend appeared in the doorway. Frederica hurried forward to embrace her. "Milly, you look just the same as ever. I am *so* glad to see you!"

"And I you, Frederica," she replied in the low, melodious voice Frederica remembered so well. At forty, Miss Milliken still possessed fine, aristocratic features and a striking style, though she could never have been precisely beautiful. "You mentioned a problem in your letter, and I can see that you have been worrying of late. I suggest you come inside and tell me about it at once." She led the way to a tiny, immaculate parlour.

As always, Milly's mere presence helped Frederica to focus and marshal her thoughts. It was a practice Miss Milliken had encouraged from the time her young charge was eight years old. "Thomas has done the most dreadful thing," Frederica began after sitting down and taking the requisite three deep breaths. "Between us, I hope that we may undo it."

She went on to relate the entire situation as her brother had presented it. Her old governess listened in silence, merely nodding once or twice. When Frederica concluded, Miss Milliken fixed sharp brown eyes upon her.

"Do you wish to marry?"

Frederica blinked in surprise. "No! That is, well, I suppose I rather expected that I would marry *some-day*. I had envisioned a gentleman with whom I would share mutual interests, a growing attraction, perhaps even love. Someone like Papa, perhaps, with estates that I could help to manage, who would be a good father to any children we might have." She paused thoughtfully. "I *would* like to have children, I must admit. The girls at the village school are very dear to me, but that is not quite the same." She gave a wistful sigh.

"And yet you have never made the slightest effort to meet such a gentleman," Miss Milliken pointed out. "You refused every suggestion that you have a London Season."

Frederica grimaced. "You have told me enough about the Season for me to know that I would dislike it excessively. To be thrust into a whirl of balls and routs, paraded before countless gentlemen and then chosen by one like a prize calf...that is not what I had in mind at all. Besides, who would manage Maple Hill were I to leave for two or three months at a time? It took me hours with Mrs. Gresham and Mr. Bridges to prepare even for this visit."

"Then it would appear that Sir Thomas has come up with a perfect solution. You can scarcely expect all the eligible gentlemen in England to come to Maple Hill to be picked over at your leisure. By marrying Lord Seabrooke, you need not subject yourself to the anathema of parties and balls to find a husband." Miss Milliken's eyes were twinkling now.

"That is not what I meant, and well you know it, Milly!" said Frederica with a reluctant smile. "It is simply that I should like to have a say in whom I marry—to choose someone with whom I can be comfortable, not have him thrust upon me. I know nothing about Lord Seabrooke beyond what Thomas has told me. He sounds little better than a rake, a do-nothing man about town. And for all I know, he could be much worse than that!" She shuddered involuntarily.

Miss Milliken regarded her steadily, her expression again serious. "The unknown is always frightening," she said perceptively. "However, I must agree that it was extremely ill-advised of Sir Thomas to make such a commitment on your behalf without your consent. I would like to think that he has your best interests at heart, and indeed it may turn out so, but you dare not leave something so important as your future to chance, or to your brother's whims. Sir Thomas has not always shown the best of judgement. We ourselves must undertake to discover everything there is to know about Lord Seabrooke," she concluded decisively.

"Oh, Milly, I knew I could count on you!" exclaimed Frederica, vastly relieved. "Where shall we start? You still have numerous acquaintances in Town, do you not?"

"I do. I shall write at once to Mrs. Pomfrey, as well as to two or three others who are not so highly placed but who may be in better positions to ferret out the type of information we require. I should have some news for you in a day or two. Once we have more facts, we can decide what our next line of attack will be."

Frederica smiled at her friend's phrasing. "I doubt not your connections will uncover something about Lord Seabrooke that will force Thomas to change his mind. There must be something havey-cavey about him or he would never have agreed to this betrothal."

Miss Milliken nodded thoughtfully. "You are very likely right. That did strike me as peculiar, particularly if the man is so popular as Sir Thomas says." She stood then and said briskly, "Now, I shall show you to your room so that you may tidy yourself before tea is brought in."

Falling easily into her old habit of obedience, Frederica followed Miss Milliken out of the room, her step far lighter than it had been when she entered.

FOR FREDERICA, staying at the Milliken cottage was like being on holiday, free from her myriad duties and responsibilities at home. She suspected that over an extended period of time she would become bored with such a life of leisure, but for a day or two it was pleasant, indeed.

Miss Milliken's father was a kirdly old man who appeared to take in little of what went on about him. Although he was delighted at his introduction to Frederica at dinner her first evening there, she had to be presented to him all over again in the morning.

"Ah, yes, Charlotte has told me all about you, Miss Chesterton," he said, exactly as he had the night before. "I am delighted that you have come to pay us a visit. Do not hesitate to make yourself perfectly at home here."

Frederica responded with polite expressions of gratitude, wondering how many times this same conversation was destined to be repeated; Mr. Milliken seemingly had a memory like a sieve.

The day was spent pleasantly, in long conversations with her old friend and in painting and reading, two interests the women shared but which Frederica rarely had time to indulge at Maple Hill. Late in the afternoon, as they were companionably washing out their brushes together, a note was delivered for Miss Milliken.

Frederica watched her impatiently as she read its contents. "Is it a response to one of your enquiries, Milly?" she asked eagerly when she finished.

"Yes, dear, it is, but I fear that it is little to our purpose," replied her companion with a frown at the sheet before her. "Mrs. Pomfrey has nothing but good to say about Lord Seabrooke, and goes on at length about how handsome he is, and how good-natured. She does rather confirm his reputation as a rake, for the ladies all love him, it would seem—even the married ones." Frederica made an outraged sound and Miss Milliken regarded her sympathetically. "That will be hardly enough to dissuade Sir Thomas, I fear, for he implied as much himself."

Frederica opened her mouth to retort, but at that moment the bell rang again and a woman in fashionable attire was shown in.

"Ah, Becky!" exclaimed Miss Milliken with a smile. "Frederica, this is my friend, Becky Long. She is abigail to the Duchess of Westover. Becky, this is Miss Frederica Chesterton, the young lady I mentioned in my letter."

Mrs. Long, a tall, thin woman with a clever face, nodded politely in Frederica's direction before turning back to Miss Milliken. "I spoke to several of my sources, as you requested, and you may well be right about Lord Seabrooke," she said without preamble. "There's something more than a little odd going on at Seabrooke House."

"Ah!" said Miss Milliken in evident satisfaction. "Please elaborate."

Frederica moved to the edge of her chair.

"It seems that he's been interviewing for an assistant housekeeper. Leah Perkins, Lady Rochester's woman, told me her niece applied for the post."

Frederica sat back in disappointment. "What is so unusual about that?" she asked.

Miss Milliken directed a stern glance her way to silence her. "Pray go on, Becky."

"Well, it seems he's doing the interviewing himself instead of having the housekeeper do it, which is strange enough. But he also asked Miss Butler some very odd questions that seemed to have little to do with the duties of the post." Mrs. Long's nose twitched with disapproval.

"Such as?"

"He had her read several pages of a book aloud, for one thing, then wanted to know where she had been schooled. He also wanted to know whether she had any younger brothers or sisters."

"Perhaps he is merely looking to fill another post at the same time—perhaps that of stable-boy or scullery maid—and prefers to keep families together," suggested Miss Milliken. "Did he hire Miss Butler?"

"No, she apparently wasn't what he was looking for," replied Mrs. Long with another twitch. "What's more, she discovered that he has been interviewing for this post for several days now, and has turned away women with far more housekeeping experience than she has. My guess is it's a different post entirely that he is looking to fill, if you take my meaning."

"Yes, er, well." Miss Milliken stood up quickly. "Thank you so much, Becky. This information may prove very useful. I appreciate your taking the time to come and tell me in person."

"My sister lives in this direction, and I had planned to call on her today, in any event," said Mrs. Long. "I must be on my way, for she is expecting me."

"I don't see how that news can help me very much," said Frederica gloomily when Mrs. Long had gone. "The fact that Lord Seabrooke is choosy about his servants is not likely to carry much weight in persuading Thomas."

"Perhaps not," agreed Miss Milliken, "but we may be able to use the situation to our advantage nonetheless. I have been thinking over various campaigns we might employ to achieve your purpose, and I believe our best strategy in this case is espionage. What we need is a spy!"

Frederica blinked. "A spy?"

"Yes, someone who can get close enough to him, or at least to his servants, to discover everything there is to know about Lord Seabrooke. It's a time-honoured strategy, and just the one we need. After all, Alexan-

der the Great had his spies, Caesar his *explor-
atores*—"

"But who? How?" interrupted Frederica eagerly.
Her friend's mounting enthusiasm was contagious.

"Well, I don't precisely know," admitted Miss Milliken. "It would have to be someone we could trust
implicitly—someone who could not be corrupted by
the enemy. This may take some time...."

"We don't have time, Milly! Thomas says I am to be
married at Christmas, and I've no desire to wed a rake,
I assure you. Can we not do it ourselves? Lord Seabrooke has never seen me, after all."

Miss Milliken's eyes began to gleam. "Us, act as
spies? How intriguing. I might manage to obtain the
position, I suppose. Of course, it would be frightfully
improper for you to reside under his roof in any capacity but as his wife, so that is out of the question. Let
me see...."

"Why out of the question? No one need discover it."
Now Frederica's imagination was becoming fired with
the idea. "As I have scarcely any acquaintance in
London, it would be unlikely in the extreme that anyone I know should see me. And I can disguise myself
somehow, so that even if they did, they would not recognize me." She recalled her recent conversation with
Thomas. "It would give me a perfect chance to discover Lord Seabrooke's true character, the one he
keeps hidden from his fashionable friends. Come,
Milly, let me do it. It would only be for a few days!"

Miss Milliken regarded her onetime charge thoughtfully. Perhaps there was something to what Frederica
said. If there really were something to be found to the
man's discredit, she could be counted upon to dis-

cover it, for she had the strongest of motives. And if
there were not—well, what better way for her to get to
know her future husband? Miss Milliken nodded
slowly. "I'll see what I can arrange," she said.

CHAPTER THREE

"ARE YOU CERTAIN that you still wish to do this?" asked Miss Milliken as she opened the large trunk she had retrieved from the attic.

"Yes, yes of course!" replied Frederica eagerly. She had been able to think of little else during the past two days. Until now, her existence had been so ordered, so routine, that the prospect of spying on Lord Seabrooke had taken on the aspect of a major adventure. "Have you arranged for me to receive an interview?"

"I have. At eleven o'clock this morning. The position open is for that of housekeeper's assistant, as Mrs. Long mentioned. Your work will not be easy, I fear."

"As it was at Maple Hill?" asked Frederica mockingly.

Miss Milliken smiled. "You're right. You should be well prepared, actually. Now, we must take thought for your disguise. I believe there may be a few useful items in here."

Frederica looked in surprise at the jumble of things in the trunk. "Gracious! Wherever did you come by wigs and paints, Milly? You never mentioned a connection with the theatre."

"Nor shall I now," said Miss Milliken dampingly. "These things were given to me. Sit here at my dressing-table and let us see what we can do."

Still burning with curiosity, Frederica sat down to face the mirror. She knew very little about Milly's past, she realized. It had never occurred to her before to wonder what she had done before coming to Maple Hill. Certainly, her father would never have hired a former actress as a governess, nor could she imagine the strictly proper Miss Milliken in such a profession. Still, she did not quite dare to probe further. "What will you do with that?" she asked instead, indicating the thick brown pencil her friend had pulled from the trunk.

"I had thought we might give you freckles. Hold still, now." She worked in silence, dusting Frederica's nose and cheeks with remarkably realistic-looking freckles. "What colour hair would you like?" she asked when she was done.

Frederica looked over the choice of wigs "The blond one is lovely, but I suppose I would be less noticeable in the brown." Miss Milliken nodded in agreement and helped her to fit the nondescript wig over her profusion of coppery curls.

"Now we must do something about your eyes. They are far too striking to be easily forgotten."

Frederica glanced at the mirror in surprise. She had never given a thought to her eyes before, but she supposed it might be true that that deep shade of green was unusual. Wide and thickly lashed, they tended to dominate her small, heart-shaped face.

"How about these?" asked Miss Milliken, holding up a pair of spectacles, fitted with clear glass, that she had fished out of a flat box in the bottom of the trunk. Frederica put them on.

"What do you think?" she asked.

"I suppose it will have to do." Miss Milliken scrutinized Frederica's still-trim figure with some misgiving. "You could wear padding to make yourself appear plump," she said, "but that might make your movements awkward."

Frederica grimaced. "I'd rather not. I should think padding would be most uncomfortable. I believe the changes we've wrought already are quite sufficient," she said, examining herself closely in the mirror. "Why, Thomas himself would not recognize me like this, I daresay. I vow, I scarcely recognize myself!"

"Your eyes are the hardest to disguise," said Miss Milliken, regarding her critically. "You must remember to wear the spectacles at all times. Yes, I think you'll do. The references I have collected should enable you to secure any *respectable* position Lord Seabrooke is looking to fill. Otherwise, well, we must hope that the freckles and spectacles will provide enough protection."

"Protection from what?" asked Frederica innocently.

Miss Milliken hesitated. "From improper advances," she finally said. "I suppose you should know that Mrs. Long thought it probable that Lord Seabrooke was looking for a young woman to perform completely different duties from those of assistant housekeeper. To be blunt, she felt that he may be looking for a live-in mistress."

"Oh!" Frederica's cheeks grew hot beneath the concealing freckles. "I—I had not thought of that!" She rallied quickly, however. "But if that is the case, surely it will be enough to convince Thomas. He can scarcely expect me to marry a man who would engage a mistress to live in his very house!" She glanced again at her reflection. "And you are right—I scarcely look *that* part. I should be safe enough."

Miss Milliken devoutly hoped so.

LORD SEABROOKE chafed at spending yet another morning at home when he would far rather be looking over the new Thoroughbreds Tattersall's had got in just yesterday. With the settlement he had received from his betrothal to Sir Thomas Chesterton's sister, he could well afford to replace the old hack he had been riding for the past year. In fact, he was finding his sudden wealth a boon in ways he had not foreseen.

No longer did he have to send his valet to pawn one of the few remaining pieces of his mother's jewellery every time he wished to purchase a new coat. Nor did he have to content himself with a single stringy cutlet for dinner each night before going out to the gaming hells in hopes of picking up a few pounds to see him through the next week. Now he could afford decent meals, served in the elegant dining-room that he had previously used only for entertaining. He had been able to hire a butler, to the great relief of his valet, who no longer had to double in that capacity, as well as a footman and two new maids to assist his long-suffering housekeeper.

It was another, very necessary, addition to his staff that kept him at home this morning. He had thought it a clever idea to advertise for an assistant housekeeper to keep the world in the dark as to his real requirement, but that pretence was making it deuced difficult to find the right woman for the job he had in mind. Mrs. Abbott had told him last night that she could not continue with things as they were for much longer, and he knew that she was right. He fervently hoped that this next applicant might be what he was looking for.

CLUTCHING HER SHEAF of false references, Frederica let fall the knocker at Lord Seabrooke's imposing Town house. The door was opened at once by a portly butler who looked down his nose at her.

"I am Miss Erica Cherrystone, come to apply for the post of assistant housekeeper," she said, using the name she and Miss Milliken had agreed upon. "I have an eleven o'clock appointment with Lord Seabrooke."

"Of course, miss. Right this way." The butler motioned for her to precede him, with a gleam in his eye that made Frederica unaccountably nervous. "His lordship is awaiting you in the library."

For a moment Frederica considered retreating, but quickly chastised herself for being such a craven. If she allowed herself to be frightened by the man's butler, she would never manage a confrontation with Lord Seabrooke himself! Reminding herself why she was there, she lifted her chin and opened the library door.

Gavin put away the watch he had been checking as the door opened. This one was punctual, at least. As she crossed the room towards him, he doubtfully examined this newest applicant. The girl was unremarkable, her mousy brown hair caught up in a conservative chignon and her serviceable grey gown years out of fashion. In spite of the spectacles, which lent her a studious air, he thought she looked rather young for the position of responsibility he had in mind.

"Pray have a seat, Miss Cherrystone," he said with a sigh. He feared that this one would be no better than the others. "You have references, I presume. May I see them?"

"Of course, my lord," she replied. At her voice, Seabrooke looked up sharply.

"Would you be so kind as to read me a passage from that book on the table beside you?" he asked as she proffered the papers.

Showing none of the surprise that previous applicants had evidenced at the odd request, Miss Cherrystone picked up the volume and opened it. "Any passage in particular?" she asked.

"You may start at the beginning. I shall tell you when to stop," he replied. He picked up the references she had brought and leafed through them as she read the opening paragraphs of Walter Scott's latest novel. "That will do," he said before she could turn the page. "Your speech is rather better educated than I would have expected from your background." He indicated the pages in front of him.

"I was raised in a genteel household, my lord," said Frederica, glad that Milly had thought of a story to account for that apparent anomaly. "It was not until my parents died that I was forced to seek work. As a girl, I received an excellent education."

"Ah, yes. Well, that would explain it."

Lord Seabrooke leaned back in his chair and finished reading through the references while Frederica studied him thoughtfully. She had to admit that he was every bit as handsome as she had been told. Thick waves of chestnut hair fell carelessly across a noble brow, his features were aristocratic without appearing harsh, and his eyes were a startlingly bright blue. She wondered, though, where he had come by his reputation for charm. Perhaps he did not deign to waste it on the hired help, she thought sourly.

Just then he looked up from the papers and smiled. *Oh!* She fought the urge to respond with a melting smile of her own, keeping her face prim and rigid.

"Miss Cherrystone, I believe you may be just the person I have been looking for. Tell me, can you be discreet? The person I hire for this position must be able to keep her own counsel."

"Discreet?" Mrs. Long's suspicions came surging back to her mind. "I am no gossip, if that is what you mean, my lord," she said carefully.

Lord Seabrooke rose and came around the desk to sit next to her, revealing a slight limp as he traversed the short distance. Placing one hand on the arm of her chair, he leaned towards her confidentially. Frederica became aware of the clean, masculine scent of him. "You see, Miss Cherrystone, the post I wish you to fill is not precisely that of assistant housekeeper, in spite of my advertisement."

"It...it isn't?" she asked weakly. She knew that she should be rejoicing that she was obtaining proof of his debauchery so easily, but somehow his close proximity was making it difficult for her to think clearly. Glancing down, she noticed the dark hairs curling on the back of his hand, a hand that appeared remarkably strong.

"No. It is a position of far greater responsibility and ... delicacy."

"I, ah, I see." Frederica tried to force her brain to work. She must get an open admission from him, something that she could take to Thomas. Once she had that, she could leave. "How...how delicate?" she managed to ask, her heart beginning to pound. Milly would never have allowed her to come alone if she had known how right she was, Frederica was certain.

Lord Seabrooke moved even closer, lowering his voice. "I would prefer that the precise nature of your duties remain hidden even from some of the other servants, at least for the present."

"And pray, just what are those duties to be, my lord?" she asked in a high, breathless voice that sounded quite different from her natural one.

The earl drew back slightly, regarding her closely through narrowed eyes. He nodded then, as though reaching an inner decision. "What would be your feelings towards an illegitimate child?" he asked abruptly.

Frederica gasped and sprang to her feet. "It is the outside of enough that you wish to hire a...a fancy woman in the first place, my lord. But that you would actually *plan* for *children* to result from such a union..." She headed for the library door. "I believe I have heard quite enough, Lord Seabrooke," she said scathingly over her shoulder. What could Thomas possibly say in defence of that ridiculous betrothal now? She had all the proof she needed.

With two long strides, Lord Seabrooke placed himself between her and the door. "Miss Cherrystone, I'm not sure what bee you have in your bonnet, but I beg you to sit down and hear me out. I'll not have you leaving in this state of mind, to spread scandal about the streets of London when I have been at such pains to keep this quiet."

"Scandal! You deserve to have scandal spread about you!" exclaimed Frederica. She was so angry that she was near tears. How dared he betroth himself to her and then advertise openly for a mistress! "Pray let me pass, sir. I will not remain here to be insulted."

To her astonishment, Lord Seabrooke began to laugh. Far from stepping out of her way, he took her hand in his, leading her back to her chair. She pulled against his grip, but her strength was no match for his.

"Let me go!" she panted. "I'll have the authorities on you for this!" She was afraid to struggle too violently, for fear that her wig might be knocked askew. What would it do to her reputation to be discovered here, in such a situation? Thomas might well insist on her marriage as a result, she realized.

Still chuckling, the earl pushed her firmly into the chair. "Sit, Miss Cherrystone," he said, and there was an edge of steel under the laughter that kept Frederica from immediately disobeying him. "You are labouring under a misapprehension, and I intend to clear it up. I would never dream of insulting a paragon such as yourself, I assure you."

"But... but you said—"

"I phrased things poorly, I must admit. Now hear me out, I beg you." He again seated himself behind his desk and picked up her references. "I see here that you had charge of Mrs. Henderson's children for a time," he said, as though their interview had never been interrupted.

Frederica nodded uncertainly. Not knowing what Lord Seabrooke was really looking for, Milly had provided her with quite a variety of references, though she was careful not to claim any skills for Frederica that she did not possess. Certainly she had ample experience with children after her work with the village school, though she could not imagine why that should be important to an unmarried man like Lord Seabrooke.

"I have recently become the guardian of a child, a little girl, four years of age. Her antecedents are, ah, dubious, but I wish to provide her with the upbringing of a young lady of Quality. My housekeeper has found herself unequal to the task of caring for the child in addition to her other duties, nor does Mrs. Abbott, though an admirable woman, have the, ah, background I would wish the child exposed to. For the present, I would prefer that the child's residence here, indeed her very existence, not become public knowledge. Of course, this has made it exceedingly difficult to find the proper person to care for her. I could scarcely advertise for a nanny or governess, could I?" He gave Frederica a wry smile.

This time she felt no inclination to smile back, though the truth was not quite as reprehensible as she had first thought. Still, it was bad enough. He wished her to care for his illegitimate child! Doubtless, he wanted the child kept a secret so that his wealthy fiancée would not hear of it and cry off. Although she could see the irony in the situation, somehow she was not tempted to laugh.

"I suppose not," she replied through clenched teeth.

"I realize that being nursemaid to such a child may not exactly suit your notions of what is proper, Miss Cherrystone," Lord Seabrooke continued, "but then, if it did, you would not be the sort of person I want." That disarming smile was still on his face. "Can I at least prevail upon you to meet Christabel before leaving in a huff?"

Frederica considered. Would Thomas find an illegitimate child in residence under Lord Seabrooke's roof reason enough to cancel her betrothal? Possibly not. He had already admitted that the man had a reputation of sorts, and whatever incident had led to this child's conception must have occurred nearly five years before. Distasteful as it seemed, she needed to discover more. Forcing her lips into a stiff smile, she met Lord Seabrooke's bright blue gaze.

"Very well, my lord, if you insist."

"Excellent!" He was beaming now. "She should be almost ready for her midday meal. This way, Miss Cherrystone."

Frederica silently followed him from the room, trying not to let her eyes linger on the broad shoulders or long legs in front of her. His limp was scarcely noticeable now. The man's clothing was impeccable, and of fine workmanship. He certainly didn't dress as though he were in need of money, she thought reluctantly.

"I must say, I had nearly despaired of finding anyone suitable," he said as he led her up the staircase at the back of the hall. "You wouldn't believe the accents and manners I've had to endure in the course of these interviews. As soon as you opened your mouth, I knew you were the very person I had been seeking."

"I haven't accepted the position yet, my lord," she reminded him severely. "And surely an accent should not be the first consideration when evaluating a person's suitability to raise a child. I should think temperament and experience would enter in as well."

"The experience you apparently have, and after our little altercation in the library, I suspect your temperament is all I could wish. You appear to have very strong views about right and wrong, and no difficulty in expressing them. I have no doubt you are well equipped to mould a young mind." He gave her a sidelong glance, his eyes twinkling.

"Indeed," was all she replied. She would *not* allow herself to be charmed by him!

Finally, after two more flights of stairs, they reached the very top of the house. "Here is the nursery," he said, opening a door on the right. "Christabel, there is someone here who wishes to make your acquaintance," he called out as they entered the room.

A spindly woman of advanced years came forward to greet them, her back as straight as a ramrod. "She's been a rare terror this morning, my lord," she told the earl at once. Her shrewd grey eyes assessed Frederica as she spoke. "I've been trying to get her out from behind the clothes-press for half an hour, with no success. She's playing one of her silly games, and tells me it is her cave or some such thing. I have a thousand more important things to do than coax a sulky child, I can tell you!"

"Very well, Mrs. Abbott, you may go about your other duties. Miss Cherrystone and I shall see what we can do." He waited until she was gone before turning to Frederica. "Mrs. Abbott is a gem of a housekeeper, but I fear that she hasn't the energy or the time to keep up with Christabel. Nor does she appear to have a natural rapport with children, never having had any herself."

"Where *is* the child, my lord?" asked Frederica curiously, glancing around the large chamber. A few toys and books were arranged on two high shelves in regimented rows, and a small table was neatly set for a meal. A little bed in the corner was smoothly made, and not a speck of dust or a scrap of stray clothing was to be seen. It seemed to her a cold, sterile excuse for a nursery.

"Behind here, I presume," replied Lord Seabrooke, crossing to a large clothes-press in the corner
opposite the bed. Looking behind it, he said, "Come
out at once, Christabel. I want you to meet Miss
Cherrystone."

In response, there was a high-pitched growling noise
from behind the clothes-press, but no Christabel
emerged.

"May I try, my lord?" asked Frederica. In spite of
her misgivings about the situation, she could already
feel stirrings of sympathy for a child forced to live in
these barren surroundings.

At his nod, she came forward and peered behind the
enormous piece of furniture. She could see a small figure crouched in the corner at the other end. "Christabel?" she said tentatively. She was greeted by the same
growling sound as the earl had been. Drawing back in
mock alarm, Frederica exclaimed, "Oh, my! There's
a bear back here! It's hiding deep in its den, my lord!"
The growling grew fiercer.

"Perhaps we can lure it out with a big piece of
meat," she suggested. Picking up a biscuit from the
table, she held it where Christabel could see it. "Here,
bear, I have some meat. Please don't eat me!"

The growling changed to a giggle, and a little girl in
a rumpled pinafore emerged. She brushed back tousled golden curls and looked up at Frederica with
enormous, clear blue eyes. She was the loveliest child
Frederica had ever seen. "I'm a wolf, not a bear," she
informed her with an impish smile.

"Oh, yes. I can see that now," said Frederica seriously. "Will you take this meat instead of my arm, Mr.
Wolf?"

Christabel giggled again and took the biscuit from her. Instead of eating it however, she held one tiny hand out to Frederica. "Are you going to be my new nanny?" she asked, gazing wistfully up at her with those luminous eyes.

"Miss Cherrystone?" prompted Lord Seabrooke when she did not answer at once.

Frederica knelt down, never taking her eyes from the child's face. "Yes, Christabel," she said softly. "I'm going to be your new nanny."

CHAPTER FOUR

"So you see, Milly, it *is* a respectable position, if rather unconventional. I believe it will serve my purpose admirably. It is really rather amusing now to remember what we suspected." Frederica took a sip of her tea. "I am to start tomorrow, so we must decide which of my things—and yours—will be appropriate for me to bring along." She had just finished relating the entire story of her interview with Lord Seabrooke and her acceptance of the post of nanny-cum-assistant housekeeper.

Miss Milliken frowned. "I am not certain I should call it precisely respectable, Frederica. If you consider how the child came into the world—which I would prefer you *not* do, actually—"

"It is scarcely poor Christabel's fault, Milly," said Frederica reprovingly. "She is the sweetest child, and simply starved for a bit of attention and amusement. After all, she had no say in the matter, and it seems most unfair that she should suffer for the sins of her parents."

"You are still very innocent, Frederica," said Miss Milliken with a sigh. "It may not be fair, but it is the way things are in the world. Darling though she may be, your little Christabel will never be accepted by Polite Society. The best she will be able to aspire to is a post as an upper servant. And there, I fear, her looks will be against her if she retains the promise of beauty you claim she possesses. A much worse, if more luxurious, fate may well await her."

It took Frederica no more than a moment for Miss Milliken's meaning to become clear. "Oh, no, Milly!" she cried, aghast. "That will never be, I am determined. With me there to guide her, to show her right from wrong, surely—"

"Frederica, are you not forgetting that yours is merely a temporary post? That your real purpose is to discover enough about Lord Seabrooke to persuade Sir Thomas to let you off marrying him? Or have you changed that plan? I will admit that as Lady Seabrooke you may well have a lasting influence on the child."

Frederica bit her lip in chagrin. "Of course you are right, Milly, and I *had* forgotten, so taken was I with Christabel. But I fear that Lady Seabrooke will have little say in the matter, no matter who she is, for it is apparent that Lord Seabrooke intends to keep Christabel's existence a secret from her."

"But my dear, you already know about her," Miss Milliken pointed out gently.

"Of course. But I do *not* intend to become Lady Seabrooke! I thought you agreed with me on that point."

"I thought I did, too," said Miss Milliken so softly that Frederica did not hear her.

EARLY THE NEXT MORNING, Frederica arrived at Lord Seabrooke's residence with a small trunk she and Miss Milliken had packed with items suitable for an upper servant in an aristocratic household, along with a few things Frederica had brought for Christabel. As before, she was admitted by the stout butler, whose manner was noticeably more friendly than it had been the previous day.

"So you're to be the new girl, are you, Miss Cherry-stone?" he said with a suggestive grin as a footman carried in her trunk. "Mrs. Abbott will be glad of your help, I don't doubt, and I can't say as I'll mind having a pretty young thing like yourself about the house, either."

Frederica smiled nervously and touched the bridge of her nose to reassure herself that her spectacles were in place. "You flatter me, I'm sure, Mr., ah . . ."

"Coombes," he supplied. "But you may call me George. This is a friendly house—very friendly."

"Of course." She put a bit more distance between them, thinking that perhaps she should have considered wearing padding, after all. With more indignation than alarm, she wondered how such a man had managed to secure such a responsible post as that of butler; certainly, *she* was more selective in the hiring of upper servants! "I'd best follow my trunk upstairs now," she said politely, and hurried to catch up with the footman, leaving Mr. Coombes and his leer by the front door.

Her room adjoining the nursery was small but well furnished, she found, with a pleasant prospect of the back garden from its single window. Frederica waited a few minutes for someone to come and unpack her trunk before the realization hit her that the new nanny would almost certainly not be assigned her own maid. Doubtless there were other privileges she had always taken for granted that she must learn to do without for the duration of her stay. The experience would likely do her good, Frederica thought with a smile as she opened the trunk and began to unpack.

She was putting away the last few items of her absurdly small wardrobe when she heard a tap at the door to the nursery. Opening it, she discovered Christabel with a little bunch of daisies in her hand.

"Mrs. Abbott says I am to come to you now. I'm glad, because you like to play and she doesn't. These are for you." She held up the flowers with a confiding smile.

"Why, thank you, Christabel," said Frederica warmly, touched by the simple gesture. "Did you pick them yourself?"

The little girl nodded. "Mrs. Abbott let me go into the garden before anyone else was up this morning. Do you like them?"

"They're lovely. I'll put them here in the pitcher until I can find a better vase. Would you like to help me finish unpacking?"

"May I?" Christabel's face lit up. "Abby never lets me come into her room."

"Well, you may come to mine anytime you wish." Frederica gave the child a quick hug. "I know we are going to be very good friends." Christabel returned the embrace with an enthusiasm that told Frederica that she had been hugged far too seldom. Frederica had brought along a variety of items to supplement the meagre collection of toys in the nursery, and Christabel thanked her enthusiastically as each was revealed. It was obvious that she had never been used to having much.

"Now, what would you like to do this morning?" Frederica asked when they had closed the last drawer, already good friends.

"Oh, I forgot. Abby wants me to say that she needs to talk to you right away. She'll be here in a moment, I think." As she spoke, the hallway door to the nursery opened, admitting the housekeeper. Frederica went into the nursery to greet her, with Christabel in tow.

"Why don't you draw me a picture while I speak with Mrs. Abbott?" Frederica suggested. She pulled a tablet of drawing paper and a box of pastels from the stack of things she had brought along for Christabel and settled her at the nursery table. Frederica and Mrs. Abbott then seated themselves at the far end of the room. "Christabel said that you wished to see me?"

"Yes," replied the housekeeper. "There are certain rules his lordship wishes you to understand, before you inadvertently break them." She looked past Frederica to the happily occupied Christabel. "You do seem to have a touch with children, miss. I never thought to distract her like that."

But Frederica's attention had been caught by Mrs. Abbott's previous statement. "Rules?" she asked sharply. "What sort of rules?"

"I believe his lordship told you yesterday that he does not wish the child's presence in this house to become common knowledge. To that end, she is not to leave the nursery except when it is least likely that she will be seen."

"Do you mean that the rest of the staff is unaware of her?" asked Frederica in astonishment. "How can that be? I cannot imagine her being silent enough, even in here, to escape detection."

"Only the female servants live on this floor, and all of us know about her. Mr. Coombes and the footman do not, but should have no reason to come up here." Her expression was prim. "You will fetch her meals, and yours, from the kitchen, or Lucy, the chamber-maid, will bring them up.''

''But surely Lord Seabrooke does not think he can keep Christabel caged in the nursery forever. A child needs exercise, and fresh air!''

Mrs. Abbott pursed her thin lips. ''To tell the truth, I am not certain that his lordship has thought very far ahead. He only had the child brought to this house ten days ago. There wasn't much else he could do when her nurse left her, her mama being dead and all.''

''Oh! Poor thing!'' exclaimed Frederica sympathet-ically, glancing over her shoulder at Christabel. ''But I should say it was the least he could do, under the circumstances.'' She was not schooled enough in the ways of the world to realize that most men would ignore such a child.

''He's always been good as gold to the little mite, and to Miss Amity, too. Some may call him a bit wild, but his heart is in the right place.''

''Miss Amity is Christabel's mother?'' Frederica knew Milly would not approve of her asking, but she was here to discover all she could, after all.

Mrs. Abbott nodded. ''He always made it a point to visit her and the child two or three times a year. It fair broke his heart when she died a few months ago—right before he succeeded to the title, that was.''

So! thought Frederica. He had apparently contin-ued his relationship with the woman long after Christabel's birth—until fairly recently, in fact. But he had never married her, in spite of the child. No doubt she had been too poor to tempt him, she thought in disgust.

''He tried to keep the child's old nurse on, but she wanted more than he could afford, it seems,'' Mrs.

Abbott continued. "He even gave up his fancy women and entertainments for a time to pay rent on the house in the country after Miss Amity died, rather than neglect what he saw as his duty. When the nurse gave notice, he let the house go and brought the child here. Now that he's come about, though, I imagine he'll be his old self in no time. You know what young men are, miss."

Frederica tried not to shudder at the thought of Lord Seabrooke—her fiancé!—keeping mistresses even while he had this child and her mother tucked away in the country somewhere. This was worse than she had imagined! And as to his fortune... "You say he was without money only a month or two ago?" she asked. "Why was that?"

The housekeeper nodded and leaned forward confidentially. "It's really not my place to say, miss, but you must be able to hold your tongue or the master would never have hired you. The Alexanders were not a rich family. Master Gavin's father never had much, being the younger son, and what he did have he gambled away. I'd say it was a mercy he went to his reward before he could pauper his son completely."

"I take it you've been with the family for quite some time," observed Frederica. Mrs. Abbott was proving to be a valuable source of information, indeed.

"Since before Master Gavin—that's his lordship now—was born, miss. I came as housekeeper soon after his parents married, back when his grandfather, the 4th earl, was alive. Lord Edmund used to put on airs even then, I remember, the few times he visited."

"Lord Edmund?"

"Master Gavin's uncle, his father's elder brother. He and Mr. Alexander had a falling out soon after Master

Gavin came into the world. After that, Lord Edmund wouldn't have nothing to do with his brother, nor Master Gavin, neither. But it seems Lord Edmund didn't do no better, for no money came to Master Gavin with the title. Just more debts.''

"No money?" asked Frederica looking about. "But this house, the furniture, all the servants—''

"Don't you worry, miss, you'll get your wages," said Mrs. Abbott reprovingly. "His lordship's well enough off now. He's engaged to marry an heiress, I hear, and did quite well out of the marriage settlement. The child, poor thing, is a bit of a skeleton in the family closet, you might say, so you can see why she must be kept a secret. I expect it's only till after the wedding.''

"I...I see." And she certainly did. So, all these fine trappings were being paid for with *her* money! He *was* nothing but a fortune-hunter! Thomas had said nothing about a marriage settlement, and she had never thought to ask. "What would happen to Lord Seabrooke were this heiress to cry off?" she enquired sharply, earning a startled look from the housekeeper at her tone. She smoothed the resentment from her features, trying to appear only mildly curious.

"There's not much left for him to sell," answered Mrs. Abbott after a moment. "This house is entailed, of course, along with the Brookeside estate, so he can't sell those. He might have to let most of the servants go, I suppose." Her face puckered thoughtfully, then cleared. "But I can't imagine that the lady would cry off. Word is she's some spinster from the country, for all she's rich, and surely any girl must count herself lucky to have landed such a handsome husband as his lordship." The housekeeper smiled fondly.

"In spite of his 'fancy women and his wild ways'?" Frederica struggled to keep her voice from shaking with fury.

"Ah, the nobility don't look at these things the way you or I do, miss. They marry for reasons that have nought to do with love, nor even respect, often as not. The young lady trades her money for his lordship's name and title, his position in Society. 'Tis common enough. No doubt she'll learn to look the other way, maybe even take a lover herself, if she's discreet. Though it's not what I'd want for Master Gavin," she said with a sigh. "He'd do much better to forgo the money and find himself a wife he can love, and who will love him in return. He's had too lonely a life."

Frederica had to bite her tongue to check all the scathing comments that rose to mind.

"But that's neither here nor there," said Mrs. Abbott with a brisk shake of her grey head. "I came to tell you what's expected of you, not give the family history. You are to take the child out into the garden only when no one else is about. Cook knows about her, and his lordship's man, of course, but not the newer servants. You may have Thursday afternoons off, leaving her with me or Lucy. When you're not busy with Christabel, you can make show of helping about the house to keep up the pretence of being assistant housekeeper, though you've no real duties there. Any questions or complaints can be sent to his lordship through me."

"I have one right now," said Frederica quickly as Mrs. Abbott stood, ready to leave. She had all the evidence she needed, but she felt an obligation of friendship, if nothing else, to Christabel. "A child cannot exist in this manner, as I said before. She must have fresh air and sunshine. I intend to take her to the Park at least twice a week, and preferably daily. You may tell his lordship I said so.''

If she were able to establish such a routine before she left, perhaps it would be continued with a new nanny. To that end, she decided she was willing to remain a few days, since she was obviously in no danger. That would also allow her to solidify her case against Lord Seabrooke, as Thomas might be reluctant to back down solely on the word of a servant.

Mrs. Abbott regarded her doubtfully. ''I'll tell him, miss, if you say so, but I can't think he'll like it. He's not in habit of being ordered about.''

Nor am I, thought Frederica fiercely. *Not by my brother, and certainly not by such a rake as Lord Seabrooke!* To Mrs. Abbott, she only said, ''I'm perfectly willing to discuss my intentions with his lordship if he finds it necessary, but I refuse to allow Christabel to suffer merely to protect his position in Society.''

Mrs. Abbott shook her head and hurried out, no doubt to report most unfavourably on the new nanny to her employer.

Frederica shrugged and went to admire the drawing that Christabel held up for her inspection.

''It's a lion,'' the little girl said, pointing out the rudiments of a mane and tail. ''Do you like it, Miss Cher ... Chest ... Chatterton?''

The child's fumbling attempts at her name sounded alarmingly like her real one, prompting Frederica to say quickly, ''Why don't you just call me Cherry, Christabel? That will be easier, I think.''

''Cherry. I like that,'' said Christabel with a satisfied nod.

"And so do I," came a deep voice from the doorway. "May I call you by that name as well, Miss Cherrystone?"

Frederica whirled to see Lord Seabrooke striding into the nursery. All that she had just learned from the housekeeper coloured her perception of him now, and she critically noticed that his eyes were slightly bleary and his hair tousled, doubtless signifying a late night on the Town.

As though to confirm her suspicion, he said, "I pray you will excuse my appearance. I have but this moment come in and have yet to make it to my bed, but I met Mrs. Abbott on the stairs and she insisted that I speak to you at once. Apparently we are at some variance over the routine to be followed."

Christabel ran forward eagerly at his entrance, and he scooped her up in a big hug. "How is my Sunshine today?" he asked while she giggled with delight.

Frederica sternly hardened her heart against the tableau before her, forcing herself to remember that he was a fortune-hunter and a rake. "I merely pointed out to Mrs. Abbott that a child, any child, needs plenty of fresh air and exercise to flourish, my lord," she said stiffly. "The rules that you have set forth do not seem to allow for that. As I told Mrs. Abbott—"

"I can see that you and I need to talk." Lord Seabrooke set Christabel down and yawned widely. "But not just now. I need a few hours' sleep before attempting to think coherently. Before I go to my bed, however, will you answer my question?"

"Question?" Frederica had no idea what he meant.

"Yes. May I call you 'Cherry' as Christabel is to do? It might help me to stand less in awe of you."

Frederica staunchly refused to smile. "As you wish, my lord," she said primly. "I shall expect to speak with you this afternoon."

"Very well. I'll send word when I'm at liberty. Good day, Sunshine, Cherry." He playfully saluted each of them and sauntered off towards the stairs, fatigue making his limp more pronounced than it had been yesterday.

What a thoroughly confusing man he was, Frederica thought, staring after him. He had an infuriating ability to disarm her even while she knew perfectly dreadful things about his character. No wonder he had such a reputation with the ladies! If his lightest word could all but make her forget her purpose, she trembled to think what effect the full force of his charm might have. Did he intend to use it to win over his wealthy fiancée? she wondered. If so, she definitely needed to have the match called off before she ever met him as Miss Frederica Chesterton, for she doubted her ability to withstand it.

"Why don't I show you how to sew buttons?" she suggested to Christabel, determined to put him from her mind, at least until their conference that afternoon.

CHAPTER FIVE

GAVIN ROLLED OVER and groaned, squinting against the blinding afternoon light that streamed in through just-opened curtains.

"I'm that sorry to wake you, m'lord, but you did say I was to call you at four," said Metzger, his valet. During his many years of service, Metzger had doubled as batman, butler, footman and, on more than one occasion, groom. Now that he was restored to a single post, he took it that much more seriously, looking after his master's dress and habits far more rigorously than did the earl himself.

"Can it be four already? It feels as though I've just closed my eyes. Very well, Metzger, I'm awake. You needn't hover," said Gavin irascibly, earning a grin from his man. "Have a message sent to Miss Cherrystone to meet me in the library in half an hour, then come back to help me with my cravat. I doubt I can manage it myself just yet."

When Metzger had gone to do his bidding, Gavin rose and regarded himself critically in the mirror. Such late nights—or early mornings, to be more accurate—were doing his looks no good at all. He had suggested to his future brother-in-law, Sir Thomas Chesterton, that he be formally introduced to his fiancée towards the end of the Little Season, thinking that would give him time to become used to the idea of matrimony. But if his antics the night before were any indication, he was as far from doing so as he ever had been.

The betrothal had seemed such a good idea at the time, a veritable godsend. Marriage to an heiress would solve his financial difficulties permanently and give Christabel a mother of sorts in one stroke. With each passing day, however, he found himself regretting that necessary decision more and more. He glanced again at his reflection and winced. If Miss Chesterton saw him like this, she would no doubt cry off at once, making his regrets needless. Nor would Miss Cherry-stone—Cherry, he thought with a brief smile—appreciate his appearance in such a state. He reached for a razor.

Half an hour later, shaved, combed and impeccably dressed, Lord Seabrooke descended to the library, looking every inch a peer of the realm. It was odd, he supposed, that the thought of the new nanny's disapproval moved him to action where the thought of Miss Chesterton's could not. Already he had found Cherry an intriguing young woman of unusual intelligence, whose severity with himself was belied by her manner with Christabel. Not only did he value her good opinion, but he discovered also that he rather looked forward to the battle of wills about to be joined.

"I'M SORRY, CHRISTABEL," said Frederica soothingly for the tenth time. "When your things were brought here, your Molly doll must have been overlooked. I promise to ask Lord Seabrooke about it when I see him this afternoon." She rocked the unhappy child in her lap in an attempt to comfort her.

Christabel had shown herself to possess a decided stubborn streak when, after her dinner, she had refused to nap without her "Molly Dolly." Patient questioning had elicited the fact that she had not had it since removing to Seabrooke House, but on this particular afternoon, she suddenly wanted it desperately.

"Uncle Gavin will know," sniffed Christabel. "He used to talk to Molly Dolly at our tea parties."

"I'm sure he will," agreed Frederica. This was the second time Christabel had referred to Lord Seabrooke by that name, but she decided against questioning the child about it. Doubtless the earl himself, and possibly Christabel's mother, had striven to hide the truth of the girl's parentage from her. "With any luck, we can have Molly here in a few days."

At that moment there came a tap at the door, and a man of middle age whom Frederica had not seen before poked his head into the nursery. "Miss Cherrystone?"

"Yes?" She looked up. This must be the valet Mrs. Abbott had mentioned.

"His lordship asks that you join him in the library at your convenience." His manner was thoroughly deferential, but Frederica doubted that those sharp brown eyes missed much. As he spoke, they took in every detail of herself and the child, as well as the nursery, now a comfortable jumble of toys and books far removed from the ruthless order that had prevailed under Mrs. Abbott's rule. While Frederica valued order highly, she knew that in a nursery it could be inappropriate if taken to extremes.

"Very well. Lucy should be up in a moment with Miss Christabel's afternoon morsel. I'll be down as soon as she arrives."

"Very good, miss." Metzger bowed out of the room.

On her way down the long flights of steps to the library, Frederica took her three deep breaths and marshalled her thoughts for the confrontation ahead. During the few hours she had spent with Christabel, she had already formed a sort of bond with the child, and was now determined to do all she could to make her lot easier. Again she could hear Miss Milliken's voice drilling her in the value of thinking through one's method of attack. With an almost militant gleam in her eye she tapped on the library door.

Lord Seabrooke stood as she entered, looking quite disturbingly handsome in a dark blue coat, matching waistcoat and crisp, snowy cravat. A few hours' sleep had certainly done wonders for him, she found herself thinking. Thrusting out her chin, she met his gaze squarely through the spectacles on her nose. "I presume we may talk now, my lord?" she asked before he could speak.

"Yes, my mind is far less fuzzy than it was this morning, Cherry," he said with a disarming grin that sent a most unwelcome tingle down her spine. "I almost feel I might hold my own in a debate with you now."

As before, she fought the temptation to smile. "We need to discuss the rules you have laid down for Christabel's routine. I find them totally unacceptable."

"So you said earlier. I thought you understood when you took the post that I wished to keep her presence here a secret for as long as possible."

Frederica was treated to a hint of that steel she had detected in him at their first meeting, but she was undeterred. "I quite understand, my lord, but you must realize that a child is not a mouse or a bird that you can cage in a corner and ignore. How long do you think it

will be before Christabel notices what you are doing
and begins to suspect that you are ashamed of her?''

The earl blinked. ''I had not thought of that, I must
confess,'' he said slowly, all trace of humour gone from
his face. ''I never want her to think that, for I am not.
It is merely that her presence here just now could . . .
complicate things.''

Frederica nodded, understanding far better than she
intended to let on. She allowed no trace of irony to
creep into her voice. ''I will respect your wishes for secrecy as far as I am able without harm to Christabel. I
propose to take her to the Park regularly, daily if possible, but I am perfectly willing to leave and return to
the house via the back entrance and to draw no attention to ourselves when doing so. Once we are in the
Park, no one will have reason to suspect that she has
any link to you whatsoever. She does not resemble you
strongly.''

A sad smile stole over Lord Seabrooke's face. ''No,
she is the very image of her mother. Why, I remember—'' He broke off abruptly. ''I suppose what you
suggest might be possible. But what of the servants? I
fear I do not trust all the more recently arrived ones so
thoroughly as I do yourself.''

The implicit compliment warmed her in spite of
herself. Slowly, she said, ''I really cannot think we will
manage to keep Christabel's existence a secret from
them for long, my lord. Could you not come up with a
plausible excuse for her residence here? I have noticed
that already she calls you 'Uncle.' Could you not pass
her off as a niece? A sister's child, perhaps?''

To her amazement, a stiff mask descended over the
earl's face. His bright blue eyes narrowed to slits and
glittered dangerously at her.

"Absolutely not! If her existence must become known, I shall pass her off as my own. My reputation in Society is already colourful enough that the disclosure of a love child will not alter it appreciably. You will oblige me by not mentioning my sister in such a context again."

Frederica's mouth had fallen open. With an effort, she closed it and tried to retrieve her composure, though her cheeks were flaming. Of course no man would insult his sister so—why had she not thought of that before she spoke? "Forgive me, my lord. I—I was not aware that you even had a sister. You are right, of course." Certainly he was right about his reputation!

"It is agreed, then. You may take Christabel to the Park whenever you see your way clear to doing so secretly. And if it should transpire that explanations must be given, you may say that she is my natural daughter. We shall hope, however, that such explanations will not be necessary."

"I shall be exceedingly careful, my lord," she assured him, pleased that she had won that victory for Christabel. He stood again, as though to dismiss her, but she quickly said, "There are one or two other matters, if you please."

"Never quit while you're winning, eh, Cherry?" asked the earl, the twinkle returning to his eyes.

In spite of her resolve to resist his charm, Frederica felt the corners of her mouth twitching. "I would be foolish to do so, would I not, my lord? These are smaller requests, however." At his nod, she continued. "Firstly, I had thought that Christabel might find her time indoors to hang less heavily if she had more to occupy her imagination and interest. At . . . at home, I have pet mice in a cage. If you do not object, I should like to bring them here—to amuse her."

"Mice? You are even more unusual a young lady than I thought, Cherry. Very well. As long as you do not allow them to run rampant or to scare the maids, you may bring any pets you wish. This is your home now, after all." The warmth of his smile made something inside Frederica tighten unexpectedly.

"Thank you. The other matter concerns a doll of Christabel's that has been misplaced, apparently during her removal to this house. She has assured me that you know of it, and I promised her to ask about it."

"That would be Molly Dolly, no doubt," said the earl with a grin. "I remember her well. A sorry-looking rag doll with very decided opinions, as I recall. Christabel cannot find her?"

"No, nor could I, and I assure you that no corner of the nursery went unsearched."

"There are some boxes that were brought with Christabel that have been stored in the attics. I assumed they merely contained her mother's things and have not gone through them, but it is entirely possible that Molly Dolly may be in one of them. I shall have them brought down this very afternoon."

"Thank you, my lord. A special toy, or even a blanket, can be of immense importance to a child of Christabel's age, particularly when she finds herself in a strange milieu. Will you wish to go through the boxes yourself?" She felt a small pang at the thought of him examining his dead mistress's possessions.

"No, no," he said quickly. "You and Christabel may do that. Is that the last of your requests?"

"For the moment," she replied, smiling at him openly for the first time. "No doubt I shall think of others as time progresses."

"No doubt." He returned her smile.

Frederica stood abruptly. "I had best get back to the nursery, my lord. Thank you for your time."

To her great surprise, the earl moved around his desk to open the door for her. "Cherry, you must always feel free to come to me with any concerns you have about Christabel—or anything else," he said seriously, looking down into her face.

For a brief moment their gazes met, and Frederica felt more strongly than ever that disturbing thrill. "Thank you, my lord. I shall," she said breathlessly, feeling as though she were agreeing to something quite different and far more important. "Good day." Turning, she hurried from the library and all but fled up the stairs to the relative safety of the nursery.

THE REMAINDER of the afternoon was spent in going through the boxes that Lord Seabrooke caused to be delivered to the nursery within the hour. Frederica had feared that the sight of her mother's things might be disturbing to Christabel, but the child, rooting ruthlessly through gowns, trinkets and bandboxes, seemed intent only on finding her beloved doll.

Frederica was surprised at the clothing the boxes contained. The dresses were for the most part quite conservative—not at all what she would have expected a fancy-piece to wear. At the bottom of one box she discovered a sheaf of letters tied together with a red riband. Love letters from the earl, perhaps? It occurred to her that the letters might very well be the tangible proof that Thomas would require, and despite a twinge of conscience at the idea of invading Lord Seabrooke's and the late Miss Amity's privacy in such a way, she tucked the stack of letters into a bottom drawer in her room.

"Molly Dolly! Here you are!" exclaimed Christabel as Frederica re-entered the nursery. "I'm sorry you had to spend all this time in a box." She held the doll to her ear. "What? You did? I'm glad." She turned to Frederica. "She says she had a very long nap and is feeling ever so refreshed now."

"I'm so pleased that Molly did not suffer from her experience," said Frederica, coming forward to shake the cloth hand that Christabel held out to her. "I'm honoured to make your acquaintance, Molly Dolly."

Christabel bent her golden head to the doll's face again. "She says you are very pretty, Cherry, and she likes you. And she wants to know if she may share my supper tonight."

"Certainly she may. I'll set a place for her at once."

Lucy brought up the evening meal a short time later, and after she had gone Frederica asked, "What does Molly like best for her supper?"

"Oh, candies and cakes, Cherry! That is all she eats."

"That doesn't sound very nourishing. Are you certain she would not prefer some bread and milk first?"

Christabel shook her head firmly. "Molly Dolly eats only sweets, and she is never ill."

"I see that Lord Seabrooke was right. Molly has very decided tastes." She placed one of her own cakes and one of Christabel's in front of the doll.

"Could she not have extra cakes just for her?" asked Christabel with a trace of disappointment.

"I'm afraid tonight we shall have to share," said Frederica, hiding a smile at the child's tactics. "Perhaps tomorrow we can convince Cook to send a few extras." Christabel was certainly not lacking in intelligence, she thought, wondering how often Molly Dolly had successfully doubled her pastries in the past. Surely a better future could be contrived for the girl than the bleak one Miss Milliken had painted!

OVER THE NEXT FEW DAYS Frederica established a routine with Christabel, discreetly leaving the house after breakfast for an hour or two in Hyde Park before it become crowded. As Seabrooke House was situated on Upper Brook Street, only a short distance from the Park gates, there was no need to draw unnecessary attention to themselves by taking a carriage or hackney.

After an early dinner, Christabel customarily napped while Frederica read in her room or went downstairs to preserve the fiction that she was Mrs. Abbott's assistant. She found, on those occasions, that there was indeed much she could do to help, for the Seabrooke household was in sad disorder. Indeed, Mrs. Abbott seemed more than grateful for her suggestions regarding the management of the establishment. Christabel then had lessons and games until supper, after which she retired for the night, leaving Frederica at liberty until her own bedtime.

During those first days, Frederica saw little of Lord Seabrooke beyond his daily visit to the nursery and an occasional glimpse of him setting out in his carriage or on horseback as she and Christabel returned from the Park. Fortunately, none of the downstairs servants had yet espied them on their way in or out. Frederica knew

that she should give Lord Seabrooke notice so that
Christabel might have another suitable nanny as soon
as she left, but she was so enjoying her time with the
child that she was loath to end it.

One symptom of her reluctance to leave was that she
had yet to read through the letters she had secreted in
her dresser drawer. She told herself each evening that
she was too tired, or that the candle was not bright
enough, but those factors, oddly enough, did not keep
her from perusing books gleaned from the library
downstairs.

It was after exchanging one volume for another
during Christabel's afternoon nap that Frederica decided to have a look at the rest of the house. Thus far,
she had seen little but the library, nursery and kitchens. Lord Seabrooke was out, she knew, for she had
seen him leaving earlier when she had happened to look
down from the nursery window. Walking softly so as
not to attract attention from the other servants, most
especially the leering butler, she peered into the other
rooms on the first floor.

There was a large parlour, obviously intended for
entertaining on a lavish scale, that boasted a piano-
forte and a harp. Frederica had been used to practis-
ing frequently on both instruments at Maple Hill, and
it was with an effort that she refrained from touching
them. The dining-room was easily spacious enough to
seat forty guests, and the ballroom at the rear of the
house was of noble proportions, if in need of a fresh
coat of paint.

As she examined each room, Frederica automatically catalogued the changes she would make in the
decor if she were mistress of the house: lighter colours
in the dining-room, fresh curtains and matching up-

holstery in the parlour, gilt on the ballroom plaster-
work. Yes, Seabrooke House had the potential to be
one of the finest in London, she thought.

Opening another door, she saw a long, well-lit room
with paintings hung along either wall. "Ah, the family gallery," she murmured to herself. "I wonder what
skeletons I might unearth here?" Letting herself quietly into the room, she walked slowly down its length,
stopping to admire an occasional portrait or to read the
identifying plaque below.

One painting, in particular, of a beautiful young
lady, drew her eye. It was bathed in light from the
window opposite, and she paused to gaze at it in
delight. The painting could not be very old, she
thought, judging by the style of the lady's gown. As she
examined the face before her, she was struck with a
sense of familiarity. Surely she had seen those soulful
blue eyes, those bright golden curls, before?

Realization hit her like a splash of cold water. It was
Christabel's face, grown up, that looked out at her
from the painting. Had not Lord Seabrooke said that
she was the very image of her mother? What effront-
ery to hang his mistress's portrait in the family gallery! To be certain, Frederica leaned closer to read the
plaque.

Amity Alexander.

Alexander? But surely, she thought, that was Lord
Seabrooke's family name! Had he married the woman,
after all? Suddenly she remembered their conversation in the library, his outrage at her brash suggestion,
and comprehension dawned. No, he had not married
her. Miss Amity, Christabel's mother, had not been
Lord Seabrooke's mistress at all. She had been his sister.

CHAPTER SIX

FREDERICA STARED BLINDLY at the painting before her as she tried to adjust her thoughts to this unexpected revelation. Her first feeling was one of profound relief; Lord Seabrooke was *not* the villain she had thought him. Instead of attempting to hide his illegitimate child from the world, he was protecting his dead sister's name from censure. Seen in this new light, his actions appeared almost honourable.

She shook her head slightly. Honourable? Lord Seabrooke was a debauched rake, as evidenced by his appearance three mornings previously. An unscrupulous fortune-hunter, he had used his practised charm to dupe a gullible young man into signing away his sister's fortune—a fortune he was already spending! No, in spite of his charity towards his poor orphaned niece, Frederica could not call him honourable.

But she now had a problem. With her primary accusation against him done away, she was no closer to proving the earl a scoundrel than she had been at the outset. He was a fortune-hunter, of course, but she rather doubted that an aging housekeeper's word on that would be enough to invalidate a marriage contract. Surely there must be financial records about the house that would provide more tangible proof? Frederica nodded grimly. The library, where Lord Seabrooke had his desk, would be the place to start her search.

She had just reached the library door when she heard the earl's firm footsteps behind her. Whirling, Frederica held up the leather-bound volume she had obtained earlier. "I was merely coming to exchange a book, my lord," she began, when a cry from the stairway stopped her.

"Cherry! Where are you, Cherry?" came Christabel's high-pitched, childish voice.

"Oh, dear!" exclaimed Frederica. "I am sorry, my lord—I thought Lucy was with her."

Lord Seabrooke looked annoyed, she thought, as well he might. But then, she had warned him how difficult it would be to keep a child forever quiet. Still, she hurried to the stairs as quickly as she could, hoping to minimize the damage. The earl followed.

"Christabel, you know you are not to leave the nursery alone," Frederica admonished the child, seeing her little face peering round the first landing.

"But, Cherry, I was lonely," said Christabel petulantly. She had obviously just awakened, and was still disheveled from her nap. "Why am I not allowed on this staircase?" she asked. "It is ever so much grander than—" She broke off with a cry as she lost her footing and fell.

Lord Seabrooke jumped forward, but Frederica was closer. With a speed she didn't know she possessed, she took the stairs two at a time and caught Christabel before the little girl had fallen more than two or three steps. Sitting down abruptly on the top stair, she cradled and comforted the frightened, sobbing child in her lap while the earl looked on, his expression unreadable.

At that moment, Lucy came hurrying down the stairs. "Oh, miss!" she exclaimed breathlessly. "I only stepped out for a minute, but—" She broke off at sight of the earl.

"No harm was done, Lucy," he said as she bobbed a curtsey, "but you may take Christabel back to the nursery now. I think she deserves a treat—oh, and give Molly Dolly one as well."

Christabel went willingly enough, cheered by the promise of a treat. Frederica rose to follow, but the earl's voice stopped her.

"You really do care about her, don't you, Cherry? I have cause to be grateful to you, I think."

"She is a very dear child, my lord," she replied, her heart still beating uncomfortably fast from the fright just past—and perhaps for another reason she chose to ignore. "I am just happy she wasn't hurt, that I was near enough to prevent it."

"Thank you," he said somberly, still regarding her with disturbing intensity.

Her cheeks flushed with embarrassment, Frederica blurted without thinking, "I find I owe you an apology, my lord." Now why had she said that? she wondered furiously as soon as the words were out of her mouth.

"An apology?" he echoed curiously. "What for?"

She took a deep, steadying breath. "For what I thought about you...and Christabel's mother. I know now that I was wrong."

"What the devil do you mean? Wrong about what?" he snapped, his pensive expression giving way to a forbidding frown.

"I—I was looking about the house and happened on the gallery. I saw the painting of Miss Amity Alexander—your sister, I presume. The resemblance between her and Christabel was quite striking, as you had said." She braced herself, expecting an outburst. Why had she not held her tongue?

The earl glared at her icily for a moment, then let out his breath in a gusty sigh. "I suppose it was inevitable that you should find out, Miss Cherrystone. From Christabel herself, if in no other way."

Frederica began to relax. "I find it quite admirable that you should wish to raise her as your own, my lord, and even more so that you would go to such lengths to protect your sister's memory." It cost her a pang to admit that, but her sense of fairness compelled it.

Lord Seabrooke snorted. "I owe her no less, I assure you. I could be no more at fault for the ignominy of Christabel's birth if I *had* fathered her myself. It was I, you see, who introduced my sister to the blackguard who betrayed her."

"A friend of yours?" ventured Frederica.

He nodded. "A fellow officer, a captain in my regiment. Amity had always lived quietly, for we hadn't funds enough to give her a London Season," he said candidly. "I believed I was doing her a favour when I brought Peter Browning home with me on leave. Quite congratulated myself that they hit it off so well, in fact." His mouth twisted bitterly. "She was such an innocent, and I not much better at the time."

Frederica was struck by the parallel with her own situation. Why did brothers take such matters upon themselves for their sisters' sakes? Women were far more capable of dealing with such things. "He did not marry her?"

"Oh, perhaps he meant to. But he managed to get himself killed in Spain first. If I'd known what he'd done I'd have finished him before Boney's troops had the chance!"

The thought of what Amity must have suffered at the time nearly brought tears to Frederica's eyes. "How did she take the news of his death?" she asked softly.

"Not well at all. It is my belief that it broke her mind, in fact. She would never admit to Christabel's illegitimacy once she was born, and insisted on giving her Browning's name. Kept claiming they'd been married, though of course she had no proof. I did not challenge her on it, but acted as though I believed her. I made certain she had a nurse for Christabel and I visited when I could, which wasn't often." He sighed again. "The child has led a lonely life, I fear. Amity loved her, I know, but she was often ill and unable to spend much time with her, and the nurses I hired for her never stayed long." He looked searchingly at Frederica. "I am glad you are here to look out for her now."

"As am I, my lord," she replied, fighting down a pang of guilt. "She is fortunate to have you here for her, as well."

"Me?" He shook his head. "I am not much of an asset, I fear. I know almost nothing about children. You, however, are the very one to help her overcome the obstacles that lie ahead for her." A twinkle returned to his eyes. "If anyone can meet that challenge, you can, Cherry. Already I perceive that you give obstacles short shrift."

"Indeed I do," agreed Frederica, abruptly remembering her purpose here. "When I am determined upon a course, nothing can turn me from it, I assure you, my lord." *Not even your charming smile,* she added silently.

IN SPITE OF such admonitions to herself, however, Frederica found her resolve wavering later in the day. Would it truly be such a bad thing to be married to Lord Seabrooke? she wondered. He was really rather pleasant, in spite of her intention to dislike him. There was something else about him as well—an invisible quality that drew her to him, even against her will. Was that charm? Something that he turned on for any woman within his radius? She didn't know, but it disturbed her peace profoundly.

The next day was Thursday, her half day, and Frederica eagerly looked forward to visiting Milly and bringing her up to date on their campaign. Her thoughts were becoming so muddled that she felt very much in need of Miss Milliken's unclouded judgement. After tucking Christabel in for her afternoon nap, she had a brief word with Lucy, who was taking over her duties until bedtime, and went down to hail a hackney.

Frederica spent more time than she had anticipated recounting her experiences of the past few days to her old friend, for every time she paused, Milly prompted her with a question requiring yet more explanation. Gradually, she became aware that Miss Milliken was extracting more from her about her conflicting feelings than she had intended to reveal.

"What does it matter that I become flustered in his presence, Milly?" she finally asked almost crossly. "You know that I have been around few gentlemen, so it is scarcely wonderful that I should be unsettled by my first close association with one."

"So you are now willing to allow that Lord Seabrooke is a gentleman?"

Frederica let out an exasperated sigh. "You are doing it again, Milly! My sentiments about the man have no bearing on the case. I refuse to be forced to marry anyone, even if he is an angel is disguise. I thought you agreed that Thomas had no right to expect it of me."

Miss Milliken regarded her onetime charge somberly. "Your brother has a perfect *legal* right to do so, Frederica. I did not dispute that. I merely agreed that it was poorly done of him not to discover your wishes in the matter first. Of course, I would do anything in my power to prevent your marriage to a man who seemed likely to mistreat you, but from what you tell me of Lord Seabrooke, I doubt that would be the case. At worst, he might cause you occasional embarrassment, but there are few wives who do not suffer that at the hands of their husbands."

Frederica clenched her jaw. She had come half prepared to defend Lord Seabrooke to Milly, but the more her old governess took his part, the more determined she became to do just the opposite. "What of the other matter?" she asked, ignoring Milly's oblique reference to the earl's indiscretions. After all, she had no direct proof of those whatsoever. "He is undoubtedly a fortune-hunter, from what the housekeeper told me. Why, he was nearly destitute before my dowry came so conveniently to his rescue."

"It does sound as though he may have misled your brother on that score," Miss Milliken admitted. "Still, being without funds scarcely makes the man a scoundrel—and *that* is what you must prove, is it not?"

"I'm afraid so." Frederica stared at the toes of her serviceable brown shoes. "I fear that even there, his first consideration may well have been Christabel's welfare, and I cannot condemn him for that. Still—"

she met her friend's steady gaze again "—if I can find proof that he deceived Thomas about his lack of fortune, perhaps it will be enough. I believe my brother is already feeling a bit guilty over what he has done—I doubt he will require a charge of murder."

"And if Sir Thomas does agree to the call the match off? What then?" asked Miss Milliken softly.

Frederica shot her a startled look. "Why, I—I suppose I shall simply go back to Maple Hill and pick up where I left off." Somehow the prospect did not much appeal to her now. She stood abruptly. "I must be getting back. I promised Christabel that I would bring my pet mice for her to play with, and I had better fetch them." If anything, unburdening herself to Milly had left her more confused than she had been when she arrived.

WHEN THE HACKNEY drew up to Seabrooke House, Frederica saw with surprise that an unfamiliar carriage was waiting in the street. The light, elegant cabriolet somehow struck her as being a lady's vehicle, and though the earl occasionally had visitors to the house, none she had seen had been women. With liveliest curiosity, Frederica let herself into the house through the back door and proceeded quietly towards the parlour.

"I have been waiting nearly half an hour!" exclaimed a breathy, feminine voice from within. "Are you certain you don't know where I might find him? I am quite put out that he should have forgotten."

"I shall ask one of the grooms, if you wish, madam." Frederica recognized the voice as that of Coombes, the butler. "They might know."

"Why did you not do so in the first place?" demanded the lady. "Pray go at once!"

The harassed Coombes fairly shot from the parlour, nearly running Frederica down before he perceived her. "Oh, excuse me, Miss Cherry," he whispered, grasping her arm familiarly to steady himself for a moment. "I'm on my way to the stables—or anywhere else to get away from that harpy in there." He cocked his head towards the parlour door. "Don't know what the master will say about her kind visiting the house." He straightened disapprovingly then gave a suggestive wink. "Care to come with me?"

"No, thank you, Mr. Coombes," replied Frederica frostily. "I take it his lordship is not in?"

The butler shook his head. "And demmed lucky, if you ask me, though she *is* a taking piece." With another wink in parting, he disappeared through a doorway at the rear of the house.

Frederica bit her lip in indecision for a moment, then, holding the covered cage she carried behind her back, she pushed open the parlour door.

A vision of loveliness with clouds of black hair and sky-blue eyes sat at ease on the divan. One glance at the scandalously low cut of her vivid blue gown and the crimson on her lips told Frederica that this was no lady of Quality.

"Did you—?" the woman began, but on seeing Frederica she stopped, raking those perfectly shaped eyes over the drab brown figure before her. "Oh. I don't suppose *you* know where Gavin is?" she asked petulantly, with just a hint of a lisp. "Are you the housekeeper?"

"Assistant housekeeper," replied Frederica demurely, surreptitiously taking in every detail of the woman's appearance. So *this* was what a woman of easy virtue looked like! She was dazzlingly beautiful;

a life of sin seemed to have left no outward mark as yet. Moving to the far corner of the room, Frederica set down her cage of mice behind a chair and pretended to dust a table so that she could further examine her.

"Maybe you can be of more help than that dolt of a butler," said the black-haired beauty after a moment. "Gavin was to have met me this afternoon at my rooms for tea, and then we were to go for a drive. He promised last night, after my performance. Have you any idea where he might be?"

Frederica shook her head. So this woman was an actress! The fascination she felt at seeing such a creature mingled with an unpleasant sinking feeling at the thought of her spending time privately with Lord Seabrooke—her own betrothed! For a moment, as a wave of anger washed over her, Frederica forgot completely that she wanted no part of that betrothal. *How dared he?*

"Perhaps his appointment with Miss Dominique has run late," she suggested with sudden inspiration, pulling a name from a novel she had once read. "He seemed most eager to see her when he left the house."

"Dominique?" shrieked the black-haired lady, somewhat marring the china-doll effect as her features contorted with rage. "Do you mean Dominique Gaspard? That little *snake!* She knows full well Gavin is mine!"

Frederica merely shrugged, delighted that she had happened onto a name that produced such an effect. His lordship would doubtless have a difficult time explaining his way out of this coil!

"Well, I'm not budging an inch until he gets back," the visitor declared, to Frederica's secret dismay. "He'll see that Ariel Sheehan can't be cast off so easily! I suppose he means to stop payment on my carriage, as well?''

To this Frederica dared not answer. Somehow she had to persuade the woman to leave before the earl returned or he would learn that she had fabricated the story about another mistress—and would doubtless want to know why. Turning her back, she straightened a few ornaments on the mantel, working her way towards the chair where she had left her pet mice. Miss Sheehan, whose angry monologue grew more shrill by the second, scarcely noticed.

Reaching her objective, Frederica quickly leaned down and flipped open the door of the cage. Whipping off the cloth that covered it, she shooed the six mice towards the furious actress.

''All his fine promises!'' she was saying. ''And all the while he was...oh! Oh! Get them away! Where did they come from?'' Amazingly, her voice rose another full octave as she scrambled up to stand on the divan.

''I fear the house is sadly overrun by the creatures, Miss Sheehan,'' said Frederica mildly. ''I am surprised you did not see any before this. Shoo!'' She waved the cloth at the confused mice, causing them to scurry closer to the woman.

''Oh, I *detest* mice!'' she wailed. ''They are everywhere, you say? I'll not stay another instant!'' She leapt gracefully from the divan to the parlour door, making Frederica wonder if she were a dancer as well as an actress. ''Tell Gavin to come to see me when he gets in!'' she commanded from the doorway. ''I am not finished with him yet!'' With that, she turned and fled for the front door, looking nervously along the floorboards as she went.

"Oh, I think you are," replied Frederica under her breath as the front door slammed behind her. "Quite finished, Miss Sheehan." Turning back into the parlour, she began to coax the mice back into their cage, a satisfied smile on her face.

THE NEXT AFTERNOON, after ascertaining that Lord Seabrooke had gone out, Frederica hurried down to the library the moment Christabel was asleep. Yesterday's events had strengthened her resolve to find some tangible proof of the earl's duplicity to show her brother. She had happened, from the top of the stairs, to see Lord Seabrooke when he came in last night, and it had been apparent that he was the worse for drink. Doubtless he had gone to Miss Sheehan, been dismissed, and had set out to drown his sorrows, she thought scornfully. No, she could never be happy married to such a man!

Why she had chosen to wait up, peering down the winding staircase, she did not consider—nor did it occur to her that injured feelings played a large part in her anger towards the earl. She only knew that she wanted out of the betrothal more than ever.

Afternoon was generally a quiet time in Seabrooke House, the staff either busy below in the kitchens or retired to their rooms to rest. Frederica reached the library without encountering anyone. She took the precaution of pushing a chair against the door, to give her warning should anyone attempt to enter, before crossing to the desk.

Pulling open one drawer after another, she discovered quickly that Lord Seabrooke had not nearly her penchant for organization. Receipts, letters and even pound notes were jumbled together with writing paper and bills in no discernible arrangement. Her search was going to be more difficult than she had anticipated. Finally, in a bottom drawer, she found a heavy ledger. Opening it, she saw that it did, indeed, contain the accounts for the earl's estate.

Scanning it quickly with a practised eye, she realized that here was the information she needed. The book detailed the income and expenditures of Brookeside Manor and its surrounding lands for the past several years, presumably since well before the present Lord Seabrooke had come into possession of it. She shook her head at the tale it told: it appeared that the Seabrooke holdings had never been particularly profitable. If anything, matters had improved in recent months, since Gavin had taken control. Frederica frowned. There were certain discrepancies here . . . but no, she had no time to puzzle them out now.

Since she could hardly take the entire ledger as evidence, she pulled open the top drawer again to remove a few sheets of writing paper. Copies of some of the key entries would have to suffice for Thomas. As she riffled through the papers, a smaller sheet fluttered to the floor. Frederica picked it up to return it to its place, glancing briefly at it as she did so.

It was a letter, dated less than a year ago, from Lord Seabrooke's sister. Skimming its brief contents, Frederica's gaze fell on the signature: *Your devoted sister, Amity Browning.* She blinked at it, then remembered what Lord Seabrooke had said about his sister's fancy that she and Christabel's father had married.

A sudden thought seized her, making her temporarily forget her original purpose in searching the earl's desk. What if Amity *hadn't* been imagining things? Suppose she and her officer really had married, without her brother's knowledge? It could mean every-thing to Christabel—a real future, possibly even an inheritance from her father!

Quickly, Frederica replaced everything she had re-moved from the desk exactly as she had found it. Her proof of Lord Seabrooke's duplicity could wait. It mattered far more to discover whether Christabel was indeed the legitimate daughter of Amity and Peter Browning.

CHAPTER SEVEN

LORD SEABROOKE left his solicitor's office in a thoughtful frame of mind. Two days before, when he had discovered that his new resources would make possible a more thorough search of the previous earl's business affairs, he had seen it as that much more proof of his dependency on the unknown Miss Chesterton's wealth. He had left that same office feeling inadequate, even ashamed.

A man should be able to conduct essential business dealings without relying on an unsuspecting chit's dowry, he told himself. It mattered little that his attorney hoped to find holdings that might make her money unnecessary to him. The betrothal was accomplished, and he had achieved it by less than honourable means. Odd that his conscience had not pricked him so before!

His conversation with Miss Cherrystone after Christabel's near accident on his return had gone a long way towards restoring his spirits. Though she had infuriated him more than once, there was something about Cherry that always left him feeling...slightly exhilarated.

Suddenly, he recalled what Mrs. Abbott had told him just that morning. He had left the checking of Miss Cherrystone's references to her, as he did with any new servant he hired. Normally he heard no more about it. This time, however, Mrs. Abbott had found discrepancies disturbing enough that she felt it necessary to inform him of them. Most of Miss Cherry-stone's supposed previous employers resided in the country, she had discovered. The only ones in Town were the Launtons, and the housekeeper there had never heard of her.

Mrs. Abbott had not gone so far as to suggest the nanny's immediate dismissal, admitting that the young woman had been of great use both to Christabel and herself. Gavin was inclined to shrug the matter off. Cherry had shown herself more than competent at her post—she might even have saved Christabel's life! And it was patently obvious that she came from a genteel background. No doubt she had good reason to keep her past a secret, if that *was* what she was doing.

As he strolled along Bond Street, Gavin found himself hoping that she might be moved to confide in him about it. He enjoyed sparring with Cherry, and felt, after their last encounter, that something of a tenuous friendship had sprung up between them. He would not jeopardize it by questioning her. Besides, he merited reproach far more than she, and she did not appear to condemn *him*.

Of course, if he were to tell her the complete story of his betrothal, he doubted that he would continue to enjoy the spirited nanny's approbation. Drab she might be on the outside, but Cherry held very decided opinions and was not afraid to share them. He smiled to himself, remembering again her outrage when she had thought he was attempting to hire her as a mistress instead of a nanny.

That thought led him to recall the bizarre scene with Ariel last night. He had gone to see her after her performance, prepared with apologies and a small gift to atone for missing their assignation earlier in the day. Before he could so much as explain the matters of business that had kept him from her, she began to hurl accusations, as well as more substantial objects, at his head, angry out of all proportion to the cause.

At first he had thought that she had somehow heard of his impending marriage, the announcement of which he had delayed putting into the papers until Sir Thomas returned to London with word from his sister. However, her diatribe had included references to another actress, to his housekeeper, and *mice*, of all things, but not a word of his fiancée. He had not stayed to hear all of it. Growing perturbed in turn, for he had been exceptionally generous with her, he had told Ariel that he was withdrawing his patronage.

"You may seek another, more patient, protector, or you may go to the devil, for all I care," he had said coolly as he left.

She had scarcely paused in her vitriolic recital of his shortcomings, and he had closed the door behind him barely in time to avoid a flying powderbox, which being made of heavy alabaster, might well have done him an injury. From the theatre, he had gone to one of his more disreputable clubs to dampen with strong spirits his confusion over the vagaries of the female sex.

That was the trouble in associating with women of Ariel's stamp, he thought now. However polished a veneer of elegance and breeding they managed to develop, a veneer it remained, allowing occasional glimpses of the coarser stuff beneath. Considering his upcoming marriage, it was probably high time he had done with mistresses altogether, at least until he discovered how he and Miss Chesterton dealt together, he thought gloomily.

And now there was this other matter. Mr. Culpepper, his man of business, had just informed him that there was reason to suspect that Uncle Edmund had been diverting money out of the estate for some years, for purposes unknown. What he could possibly do about it, or how it could even be proved, Gavin had no idea. Nor did he see how the knowledge could benefit him. If the money was gone, it was gone, and it mattered little how his uncle had lost it.

Shrugging, the earl turned back towards the corner where his groom was waiting for him. As he climbed to the driver's seat of his new high-perch phaeton, he was assailed by another attack of conscience at the thought of where the money to purchase it had come from. He suddenly wondered if he would feel better if he were to confess the whole to Cherry and submit to her judgement of his actions. The mere thought made him feel better, though of course he could do no such thing. Chuckling to himself at the absurd idea, he whipped up his pair and headed for home.

CHRISTABEL WAS already awake upon her return to the nursery, so Frederica had perforce to delay further thought on the possibility of somehow proving her charge's legitimacy. As she had most of the morning, Christabel wanted to do nothing but play with the mice Cherry had brought her yesterday. It warmed Frederica's heart to see the child so happy and involved with them, and she was glad she had thought to bring them for her.

"What are their names again, Cherry?" Christabel asked as she reached into the cage to stroke each lightly on the back with one finger, as Frederica had shown her. She was proving herself remarkably gentle for a child of her age.

"The white ones are Pinky and Dinky," answered Frederica, pointing at them in turn. "Dinky is the smaller. The grey one is Graham, after my housekeeper at home, and the brown one is Chestnut."

"What about the spotted ones?"

"The one with the bigger spots is Patches, and the one mostly white is Freckles."

"Oh, because it looks as though he has freckles!" said Christabel delightedly. "Just as you do, Cherry, though yours are not so dark. I'll remember now!"

Frederica resisted the urge to go to her mirror at once to examine her false freckles. She had touched them up upon arising, as she did every morning, but she always worried that she would forget, or that she would accidentally rub them off during the course of the day. Wearing a disguise all the time, so exciting at first, was becoming a bit of a trial. The glasses chafed her nose and her scalp frequently itched under the heavy wig.

"Would you like to take one of them out of the cage?" she asked Christabel. "Which is your favourite?"

"Freckles," she answered impishly, wrinkling her nose. "I wish I had some, too."

They played with the mice until suppertime, when Frederica firmly insisted on having them back in their cage in the corner before Lucy appeared. "Some people aren't as fond of mice as you and I," she explained to Christabel, suppressing a smile as she recalled Miss Sheehan's reaction to them yesterday. She was burning with curiosity to know what had happened between her and the earl later, but doubted that she would ever find out.

After supper where, as had become customary, Molly Dolly received a cake of her own (which always disappeared mysteriously when Frederica turned her back), they tidied the nursery together and Frederica put Christabel to bed. At long last she was able to retire to her room to give some thought to her latest plan.

Even if a marriage had taken place between Christabel's parents, it might be difficult to prove at this late date, Frederica realized. She had very little to go on— only Amity's apparent belief that she had been Peter Browning's legal wife, a belief that Lord Seabrooke did not share. Suddenly Frederica remembered the bundle of letters she had secreted in her bottom drawer, when she had believed them to be written by the earl. Might they have been from Captain Browning instead? Eagerly, she went to retrieve them.

Frederica hesitated a moment before untying the riband that held the stack of letters together. Should she perhaps ask Lord Seabrooke's permission before reading them? It was not as though she had any real right to the information they might contain. Carrying the bundle closer to the candle, she looked carefully at the folded sheet on top. With a surge of disappointment, she realized that the handwriting was in fact the earl's, which she now recognized after her search through his desk that afternoon. This letter, at least, would tell her nothing.

Carefully, still not untying the riband, she went through the rest of the stack. No, some of those farther down were addressed in a different hand—they were not all from Lord Seabrooke! She stood, irresolute, then came to a sudden decision. This matter con-

cerned the earl far more than it did her. It was only fair
that he should be involved. Besides, it would be extremely difficult to explain to him why she had taken
it upon herself to read the letters, even if she discovered what she hoped to. Pausing to check her reflection in the mirror, she satisfied herself that her disguise
was as effective as ever before turning to go downstairs.

As she reached the first floor, Frederica saw
Coombes emerging from the dining-room with a bot-
tle of wine on a tray. He spied her at the same moment
and came towards her with a suggestive smile.

"Is his lordship dining at home tonight?" she asked
before the butler could ask whatever impudent question he was forming.

"He's just finished," Coombes replied. "He asked
me to take his port into the library. He often sits there
after dinner when he don't have other plans." His eyes
roved over her impudently as he spoke. "Were you
wanting to talk to him? Mayhap it is something *I* can
help you with."

"No, it is not. Would you ask Lord Seabrooke if I
might speak with him in the library?"

At the disapproval in her tone, Coombes pulled back
with a sneer. "Here he comes. Ask him yourself," he
said insolently, turning his back on her to saunter into
the library with his tray.

Frederica stepped towards the double doors of the
dining-room as the earl emerged. "Might I have a word
with you, my lord?" she asked quickly, before she
could lose her courage. What was it about this man
that caused her heart to race so alarmingly?

"Cherry!" Lord Seabrooke favoured her with a delighted grin. "The very person I wanted to see. Please,

join me in the library." He motioned her ahead of him as Coombes came back into the hallway. "Perhaps you would care for some sherry?"

"No, thank you, my lord." Frederica felt ridiculously pleased that he appeared glad to see her. "There is something I wished to ask you."

"Fire away," he said cheerfully, settling himself in an armchair near the fireplace and gesturing to the one opposite. He helped himself to a glass of port while she seated herself, and Frederica found her gaze irresistibly drawn to his strong brown hands as he replaced the cork.

"It . . . it concerns Christabel, my lord. More particularly, her parentage," she began tentatively, unwilling to spoil his convivial mood.

As she had feared, a slight frown creased his brow. "You're not having second thoughts, are you, Cherry? You knew about it when you agreed to take the post, and it would pain her greatly if you were to leave, now that she has grown so fond of you."

Frederica swallowed. "No, no, it is not that." Though, of course, she *would* have to leave before much longer. The thought of causing Christabel unhappiness troubled her deeply. "I was remembering something you told me the other day, about her mother."

The earl's expression relaxed. "Yes?"

"You said that she had always claimed that she and Christabel's father had married, but that you did not believe her."

He sighed. "Poor Amity. That fantasy doubtless helped to keep her from despair. I hadn't the heart to destroy it."

"But suppose, my lord, just suppose that it *wasn't* a fantasy? Is it at all possible that she and Captain Browning might have married without your knowledge?"

The earl was already shaking his head. "It makes no sense, Cherry. Why should they keep it a secret? Amity knew I would not oppose such a match, especially as I had been the one to bring them together. And why would she have said so only after Browning's death?"

Frederica could see the shadow of bitterness in his eyes again as he spoke and wished she could erase it. "But perhaps there was no opportunity for them to tell you sooner. And what about his family? Might *he* have wished to keep it hidden?"

"Amity had no cause to blush, either for her lineage or her accomplishments. She would not have shamed the highest peer of the realm!" he protested stiffly.

"Of course not, my lord," agreed Frederica primly. "But Captain Browning's family may not have had a chance to become acquainted with her sterling qualities. And what of my other question? *Could* they have managed it?"

The earl was still frowning, but he answered thoughtfully, "Our father's estate was in Northumberland, less than a day's journey to the border. But I cannot believe they could have made the trip in such secrecy."

"You do not know, though?"

"Browning and I were assigned to different regiments after I was promoted to major. I rather lost track of him after that, until I heard that he had been killed in Spain. I went home upon my father's death two months later. That is when I discovered how it was with

Amity." Rage quavered in his voice for a moment and then he sighed. "And now she is dead, as well. Everyone I ever cared for is dead. Why dredge up the past?"

"For Christabel's sake," said Frederica softly. "Think of what it could mean to her. We owe her that much, do we not?"

Lord Seabrooke met her eyes with a searching, almost tender gaze. "You really do care, don't you, Cherry?"

Frederica forced herself not to look away. "Yes, of course I do." She was only beginning to realize how much. Alarmed at the direction her thoughts were taking, she hastily cleared her throat. "Christabel has become very dear to me, my lord," she continued in a different tone. "I should like to improve her lot in life if it is within my power to do so."

The earl's smile was kind, but sad. "I am grateful for what you are doing already, Cherry. She has needed someone to care for her, to teach her as her mother would have done had she been well—had she lived. But I see no way now to discover what you hope to, even if it were true, which I doubt."

"There may be," said Frederica eagerly, lifting the letters from her lap, glad for an excuse to break away from that too intimate gaze. "When I was going through your sister's boxes to find Molly Dolly, I discovered these. Is it not possible that if she had secretly married Captain Browning, the fact might be revealed in a letter? I wanted your permission to go through them—for Christabel's sake." She met his eyes again, this time pleadingly.

Gavin regarded the eager face before him and felt an odd stirring of emotion. There was something about this girl that touched a place deep inside him. True, she was no beauty, not with those freckles, that mousy brown hair, those spectacles—though her deep green eyes were strangely compelling. It was something far more fundamental than mere appearances that drew him; an inner beauty comprising strength of character and convictions, intelligence and kindness. He found he wanted to explore the feeling further.

"We'll go through them together," he said. "For Christabel's sake."

CHAPTER EIGHT

OF THE FORTY or so letters in the stack that Frederica had found, it transpired that nearly a dozen were from Peter Browning. By reading through them in sequence, it was possible to trace the development of his romance with Amity Alexander. That there had been real affection, even love, between them was apparent—so apparent, in fact, that Frederica found herself embarrassed to be reading the effusions of this man, now nearly five years dead, to his beloved. Lord Seabrooke, it appeared, was similarly affected.

"This is making me deucedly uncomfortable, Cherry," he said as he picked up the fourth letter. "I don't know whether to be angry at Browning for writing to my sister so, or to be sorry for them both. I only know that I cannot keep from feeling as if I am prying."

Frederica nodded. "I know what you mean. If it were not of such importance to Christabel, I could never feel that we were justified in doing this. Still, it is not as though either of them can be harmed by it now." Suddenly, jarringly, she remembered that she had originally intended to read these letters when she believed Amity to be Lord Seabrooke's mistress, to turn them to her own ends. Where had her high principles been then?

"Would you prefer that I read through them, my lord, and bring anything of relevance to your attention? They will inspire no painful recollections in myself as they must for you." She could spare him that, at least.

The earl hesitated. "Perhaps it would be best," he finally said. "You may sit here, at this table, while I attend to some other business at my desk. That way you may apprise me at once of anything you find."

Frederica blinked at him in surprise. He wanted her to stay here in the library with him? But she only said, "As you wish, my lord," and settled back to reading the letter before her.

Gavin was similarly startled by his decision. It would have made more sense, he supposed, to send her back up to the nursery with the letters, so that she could read them at her leisure. He knew that he could trust her to bring the slightest clue to him in the unlikely event that she discovered one. The only explanation he could find was that he enjoyed her company. It seemed most odd, for she was not at all the sort of female who normally appealed to him, but there it was. Perhaps she simply made him feel comfortable, as a mother, a sister, even a friend might, he thought. That had to be it.

Shaking his head as though to clear it of such unwonted thoughts, he pulled open the bottom drawer of his desk and dug out the ledger containing the accounts of the Seabrooke holdings. When he had first obtained it from the estate in order to bring the entries up to date, he had glanced through the earlier pages, but had not examined them in any detail. Now, after what his man of business had said that afternoon, he decided he had better do so.

This volume summarized the receipts, debts and payments made for the Seabrooke estate over the past decade. Presumably his new steward had books containing individual entries for each month and year and for each aspect of the estate, but this was a starting point. He could always request the entire set of accounts if it became necessary. Poring over the columns of numbers, he wondered what the devil he was looking for.

Gavin had never particularly concerned himself in the financial aspects of his father's small estate, for most of it had been sold to pay off various debts before he inherited it. What little remained had been fairly easy to manage; it was largely a matter of trying to raise enough money from the surrounding farm to pay the few servants and maintain the manor house— a losing battle.

These accounts, on the other hand, implied an estate stretching far beyond Brookeside Manor itself, with numerous farm holdings, dairies, breeding stables and a whole village to work in them. He had not realized before what the Seabrooke estate had been in his grandfather's time—until only a few years ago, in fact. Where had all the money gone? There were not enough details in this summary ledger to tell him.

"Hell and damnation," he muttered under his breath.

At once, Miss Cherrystone looked up. "Is something amiss, my lord?" she asked.

"I beg your pardon, Cherry," Gavin said quickly. He had nearly forgotten her presence in the library. "I am merely trying to puzzle out my uncle's accounts and am not getting on at all. His old steward apparently used some sort of code in making his entries."

"Perhaps I can help," she offered, dabbing hastily at the corner of her eye with a handkerchief as she rose. "I have some small experience with household accounts."

Gavin smiled, imagining the little cottage with its kitchen gardens that she had no doubt been used to. "You are certainly welcome to try, but I fear these records are rather complex. They pertain to the entire Seabrooke estate, or what it used to be, at any event. Still, your assistance will be appreciated, as I cannot make head nor tail of the figures." He pushed the heavy book towards her.

Frederica was surprised to feel none of the triumph that she might have expected at being given such free access to Lord Seabrooke's financial records. She knew that she should consider this the very chance she had hoped for, to prove beyond a shadow of a doubt that the earl had betrothed himself to her under false pretenses to shore up a lack of fortune. To prove him a fortune-hunter of the basest kind. Instead, she found herself hoping that she really could help him, not only to ease his burdens, but also to win his approval. The realization was most disturbing.

Scanning the columns of figures more carefully than she'd had a chance to do before, she again became aware of some discrepancies. The notations the steward had used, which the earl had referred to as code, were very similar to those she herself used in the Maple Hill account books, and she had little trouble deciphering them. She turned a page, looking farther back in an attempt to discover when the discrepancies had begun.

"Here, my lord," she said after a moment. "Do you see? Three years ago, fairly large sums of money began to be diverted from one of the farms. Then here, six months later, he began to draw off the profits of the stables, and then the dairies, here. Was your uncle a gamester, perchance?''

To her surprise, the earl's colour deepened as though he were embarrassed at her question, but he answered readily enough. "Actually, I never knew Uncle Edmund, so I can't answer for his character. But from something I recall my mother once saying, it seems unlikely. You see, my father was quite an elbow shaker—lost a great deal to the dice, in fact—and that was apparently the principal reason for his estrangement from my uncle. I got the distinct impression that Uncle Edmund was quite disapproving of my father's penchant.''

So that was it, thought Frederica with ready sympathy. Of course Lord Seabrooke would be embarrassed by a reminder of his father's gambling. She had no notion that her words had struck even closer than that. "It does seem unlikely, then. This notation here—'' she pointed to the ledger page before her "—usually means that some sort of investment was made. If that were the case, it seems unlikely that it was a profitable one, for no money seems to have been ploughed back into the estate.''

Lord Seabrooke nodded, regarding her curiously out of the corner of his eye. Indeed, she did have some knowledge of account books! "Is there any way to tell what type of investment it might have been?'' he asked.

She shook her head. "Not from this. You would need the quarterly books to determine that, and it is possible it might not have been entered even there if it were something he was desirous of keeping from the world—if it smacked of trade, for instance. Oh!" Miss Cherrystone put a hand to her mouth.

"What is it?" he asked, moving closer to peer over her shoulder. He doubted that he would understand anything he saw on the page, but he found it oddly pleasant to be so near to her. She drew back at once, however, to regard him with wide, concerned eyes.

"My lord, is . . . is it possible . . . do you suppose . . . might your uncle have been at all sympathetic to the French?"

Gavin's jaw dropped. Suddenly it seemed blindingly obvious to him. After all, he had been instrumental in exposing numerous highly placed men who had raised or donated large sums of money to Napoleon's cause. Why had that explanation not occurred to him at once?

"My lord, I am sorry. That was a foolish thing for me to say." Miss Cherrystone looked extremely distressed and Gavin realized that his face had given his thoughts away. "It was merely—"

"No, Cherry, it is I who was a fool," he said quickly, lest she think him angry at her instead of at himself. "I cannot think why I had not considered that possibility before. As I said, I knew little or nothing of my uncle's character, so it would be foolish in me to protest that he would have been incapable of treason."

At Frederica's gasp of dismay over the harsh word, he regarded her sympathetically. "Of course, this is still mere speculation on our part. Tomorrow I shall begin making discreet enquiries. Thank you for opening my eyes to the possibility."

"It is only one of many, my lord," she hastened to assure him. "It is also quite reasonable to assume that he may simply have made unfortunate investments—or even sound ones that have not yet borne fruit. Pray do not convict your uncle until you are in possession of all the facts."

Gavin smiled. She truly seemed to care, not only about his feelings in the matter, but for his family honour. "No, of course I won't." He glanced at the clock on the mantel. "It is late. Why do you not resume your perusal of those letters on the morrow? I shall do my detective work and you may do yours, and we can meet here tomorrow evening after dinner to discuss our progress."

Though she felt her cheeks grow pink, Frederica nodded without hesitation. "Very well, my lord. Let us hope that we both shall have good news to share."

She took her leave of him and left the room, carrying the bundle of letters. Gavin continued to smile after she had gone. He was already looking forward to the next evening. But first, he had much work to do, he realized, his smile disappearing. Reseating himself at his desk, he began to map out his best course of action for discovering the truth about his late Uncle Edmund and what had been done with the Seabrooke fortune.

FREDERICA COULD feel herself trembling as she closed the door of the library behind her. How on earth, without even so much as flirting with her, could Lord Seabrooke do such things to her nerves? Taking three deep breaths, she looked up to see Mr. Coombes regarding her knowingly from his post near the front door. In no frame of mind to concoct explanations to counter his obvious suspicions, she merely nodded in his direction and proceeded to the stairs in as dignified a manner as she could manage. She was grateful that he did not seem disposed to say anything as she retreated.

Back in her room, she peeped into the nursery to assure herself that Christabel was still sleeping peacefully before settling into a chair by the candle to continue reading through the letters. Instead of focusing on the words before her, however, she found herself replaying the scene that had just occurred in the library.

Dreamily, she recalled every look, every word, that the earl had directed her way. True, he had not flirted in the least, but there had been a warmth, a friendliness, in his manner that meant far more to her than pretty phrases. Frederica realized that other than Miss Milliken, who stood almost in the position of a mother, she had never really had a close friend.

The thought brought her up short. A friend? Did she consider Lord Seabrooke a friend? Yes, she had to admit that she did. How had she allowed this to happen? She had certainly never intended to become *friends* with the earl! And how would this development affect her plan? Could she tarnish a friend's reputation in the eyes of the world—or even in the eyes of her brother— with a clear conscience?

Frederica sighed. No, she could not. In vain she tried to summon up her original resentment, her outrage, at what Lord Seabrooke had done. He *had* fooled her brother, hiding his lack of fortune to secure himself a wealthy bride. But now she was almost certain that his motives had not been completely selfish, that he had had Christabel's welfare in mind as well as his own.

He was still a rake, of course—she had met his mistress! She had to admit, though, that the memory of Miss Ariel Sheehan and her abrupt departure did not now call up anger so much as amusement—and perhaps a twinge of jealousy. At any rate, she had doubtless done a great deal to sour *that* relationship.

Still, she could not go so far as to say that she actually wanted to *marry* Lord Seabrooke. Pride, if nothing else, revolted at the idea of having her hand forced in such a manner. But how was she now to prevent it?

She thought hard. Of course, if it were to transpire that her suspicion was correct and the previous Lord Seabrooke had been a traitor to the realm, Thomas might well consider that fact enough of a deterrent. He would have no desire to be allied with such a family, she was certain, for Thomas was patriotic to a fault. Only with the utmost difficulty had she managed to dissuade him from enlisting in the recent war. It was likely Lord Seabrooke's military history that had convinced Thomas he must be an admirable man.

But Frederica could not bring herself to hope that the earl's uncle would prove to have been a traitor. Having served in the army himself, Lord Seabrooke would doubtless feel the disgrace all the more, and the thought of his pain disturbed her deeply—far more deeply than it should. Still, if there were no other way out of the match for her, this could always be the ace she held in reserve.

Attempting again to focus on the letters she held, Frederica became aware of a pounding headache, brought on by her unwelcome musings. The letters could wait. Right now she wanted nothing so much as her bed and a dreamless sleep.

WHEN FREDERICA and Christabel returned from the Park the next morning, they were both in high spirits. Christabel's were easily explained by the novel experience of feeding bread to a flock of ducks at one end of the Serpentine. Frederica preferred not to examine the cause of her own happy mood.

"I'll race you up the stairs," she said playfully to her charge after she had ushered her quickly through the kitchen, which was empty as it always was at this hour. Christabel giggled with glee and bounded up the servants' staircase with her nanny in hot pursuit. Though Frederica could easily have caught up with the child, she made a great show of trying and failing to pass her on the stairs. She knew that they were making more noise than they ought, but she was feeling strangely reckless today.

At the top of the second flight, disaster struck. Christabel, laughing and looking back at her pursuer, ran headlong into Mr. Coombes, who was coming from the servant's wing. Considerably startled, he stepped quickly back before stopping to scrutinize the disheveled little girl and the equally windblown Frederica, who had by now reached the landing.

"So, Miss Cherrystone," he said, a slow smile spreading across his pudgy face, "I see that the gossip I heard below stairs is true. The master *is* hiding one of his by-blows in this house, and you apparently helping him to do so! So much for your virtuous, prickly airs."

Frederica was aghast that he should speak so before Christabel, and it was with great effort that she restrained herself from setting him down sharply, realizing that that would likely do more harm than good.

"Good day, Mr. Coombes," she said coolly. "I see you have made Miss Christabel's acquaintance. We are on our way to the nursery at the moment, but later I should like to have a word with you." She hoped that enough of her anger showed in her eyes to dissuade him from further speech, but his smile only broadened.

"I'll be waiting right here," he said suggestively. "Hurry back."

With a gasp of outrage, Frederica took Christabel firmly by the hand and hurried her up the last flight of stairs. Something would have to be done about that dreadful man at once, or there was no knowing what stories he might spread throughout belowstairs London concerning Lord Seabrooke!

"Christabel, dear, why not build me a tower from these blocks until I return? I need to speak to Mr. Coombes for a moment." She trembled lest the child ask what a "by-blow" was, but Christabel merely nodded and began eagerly to stack the blocks. Frederica dared to hope that no damage had been done by the encounter—at least to Christabel. Squaring her shoulders, she marched back down the stairs to the waiting butler.

"Mr. Coombes," she began as she reached the spot where he stood, that odious smile still on his face, "it was unpardonable in you to use such language in front of a child. You will please refrain from doing so again."

"I daresay she'll have to get used to it soon enough," he said with unconcern. "His lordship can't keep her hidden in the attics forever—or you either, though I can see why he might want to keep *you* to himself!"

Frederica ignored that. "Lord Seabrooke has good reason to keep Christabel's presence here a secret for the present. If you value your post, I would advise you to respect his wishes in the matter."

Coombes sidled closer to her. "Oh, I can keep my mouth shut, if it's worth my while to do so. No doubt his lordship would be willing to expand the nanny's, ah, duties, to see his secret preserved." He seized her

roughly before she realized what he intended and pulled
her against him.

"How dare you?" snapped Frederica, unwilling to
scream for fear of drawing other servants to the scene.
In spite of the butler's greater strength, she felt confident of her ability to handle him. "I could have you
dismissed for this!"

"I think not, my pretty," he replied with a chuckle.
He moved his face within inches of hers. "Good but-
lers are rather harder to find than light-skirt nan-
nies!"

Remembering one of Miss Milliken's more unor-
thodox lessons, Frederica lifted one foot and brought
her heel down hard on the man's instep. He released
her with a startled howl of pain.

"You will not touch me again, Mr. Coombes! I do
not threaten idly," she informed him furiously.

He appeared nearly as angry as she, his fleshy cheeks
quivering with barely contained rage. "We shall see
who gets dismissed over this, my fine lady!" he
snarled. "When I'm done, you'll not find another post
in all of London!" He turned and stomped down the
hallway towards the main staircase, his back rigid in his
fury.

Frederica watched him go with relief. She doubted
that he would actually go to Lord Seabrooke with their
encounter, as it would present him in a far worse light
than it would her. And she doubted she would have to
endure any more unwelcome advances from the man,
either. Her only fear was that he might seek to spread
malicious gossip about the earl out of spite.

Well, if her theory about Christabel's parents proved
true, even that would be no threat, she realized. She

would finish reading through the letters that afternoon and share her findings with Lord Seabrooke that evening. Her heart lighter at the thought, she mounted the stairs to the nursery.

CHAPTER NINE

FREDERICA SLOWLY descended to the library at the appointed hour, ordering in her mind the things she wished to say to the earl. After reading through every one of the letters from Captain Browning, she felt that they supported her theory, but unfortunately offered no hard proof. She hoped to convince Lord Seabrooke to go a step further in the investigation. If he would not, she was determined to do so on her own. Proving Christabel's legitimacy was rapidly becoming an obsession with her, keeping her thoughts from other matters that might have engaged them.

She tapped lightly on the library door and opened it upon receiving an answer from within. Her careful phrasings fled from her mind when she beheld Mr. Coombes standing by the earl's desk, watching her mockingly as she advanced. Involuntarily, she met Lord Seabrooke's eye, to find a silent question there. He was looking unwontedly somber.

"Ah, Miss Cherrystone." The earl's formal tone immediately put her on her guard. "I'm glad you are here. Coombes has brought a serious accusation against you, and I have told him that I can take no action until I have heard your side of it."

Frederica glanced at the butler, then let her gaze slide away without acknowledging him. Not for nothing had Miss Milliken taught her how to administer the cut direct, though she had also impressed her charge with the very limited circumstances in which it might be appropriate. Frederica felt certain that this was one of them.

That Lord Seabrooke noticed was betrayed by a quick upward quirk of his lips, immediately controlled. Mr. Coombes stiffened perceptibly.

"Accusation, my lord?" Frederica was pleased that she managed to keep her voice perfectly calm.

It was too much for the butler. "I have proof, too, Miss High-and-Mighty," he burst out, refusing to be talked about as though he were not present. "These things were found in your room!" He gestured towards a small pile of objects on the earl's desk.

Still Frederica would not deign to look at him. Instead, she stepped forward to examine the items indicated.

"Coombes claims he discovered these things, which belong to two of the housemaids, in your chamber," explained the earl.

Gavin could not help but admire Miss Cherrystone's coolness, her refusal to be ruffled. He had been considerably startled when his butler had approached him as he left the dining-room, and even more so when he heard the man's accusations. It seemed inconceivable that they could be justified. For one thing, Coombes had never struck him as particularly trustworthy, even though he had come highly recommended. But he could not fathom what the man's motive might be to bring such a charge falsely.

"I have never seen any of these items before, my lord," said Miss Cherrystone, still without showing any of the nervousness one might reasonably expect in a servant, even an innocent one, faced with such a situation. "Nor has Mr. Coombes ever been in my room.

I'll warrant he cannot even say with any certainty where it is."

Though she addressed herself only to the earl, Mr. Coombes began to bluster in response. "It's on the top floor, of course. How could I not know, when you were running up and down the back stairs this very afternoon with that child, making enough noise to wake the dead."

"You encountered Christabel today, Coombes?" Gavin's tone was conversational, but his eyes narrowed dangerously. "Tell me, had you seen her before?"

"No, m'lord. I'd heard talk, but if you wanted to keep her a secret, it was not for me to go prying," he said self-righteously. "You'd do well to hire someone to watch her that can behave more discreetly."

The earl glanced at Miss Cherrystone, whose mouth had tightened at the words. "By discreet, I presume Mr. Coombes means someone who will accept his unwelcome advances in return for his promise of secrecy," she said acidly, for the first time admitting to having heard the butler, though she kept her eyes on Lord Seabrooke. "He threatened to have me dismissed when I refused, and this is apparently the method he has chosen." She waved contemptuously at the objects on the desk.

"Ye little hussy!" cried Mr. Coombes, his cultivated accent slipping. "No one will believe an underhousekeeper, or a bastard's nanny, or whatever ye are, over me! I never touched 'er, m'lord, I swear it!" He turned back to the earl, belatedly attempting to repair his tattered dignity.

"Thank you, Miss Cherrystone, that will be all for now," said Gavin evenly. He wanted her out of the room before he gave in to the temptation to do violence to Coombes. She left quietly and he turned on the butler the moment the door was closed.

"You will leave this house at once, Mr. Coombes," he said, his voice deadly. The thought of this man pawing Miss Cherrystone filled him with an almost unreasoning fury. "Leave an address with Mrs. Abbott, and your things will be delivered to you in the morning, along with your wages owing."

"What?" Coombes was plainly thunderstruck. "You mean to take her word over mine? Why, the little minx tried to seduce me in the back hallway!" A more observant man might have taken warning from the earl's blazing eyes, but Coombes plunged on. "Wouldn't take no for an answer, neither. She even—" He was forcefully interrupted by a shattering blow to his jaw.

"Get out." Gavin's voice quavered with rage as he glared down at his erstwhile butler. "Do not say another word, or I may not be answerable for my actions."

Coombes scrambled to his feet, anger and fear fighting for supremacy in his face. With his hand on the library door, he turned. "Don't expect me to keep yer precious secret once I'm gone, yer lordship," he sneered. "All of London will know about the brat by the end of the week. We'll see what yer fine rich bride-to-be has to say about *that!*" With this parting shot, he was gone.

Gavin waited until he heard the front door slam as well, then slowly began to relax. What on earth had come over him? He had never been especially prone to violence, though his skill was well regarded at Gentleman Jackson's. In fact, he could not recall striking another man in anger since his schooldays. Coombes was a scoundrel, of course—his final words had proved that clearly—but surely Gavin had overreacted. Why?

Cherry's face, with her wide, understanding green eyes, rose before him. That Coombes should have attempted to... Anger assailed him again. Was that it? Was he developing a *tendre* for Christabel's nanny? It seemed unlikely in the extreme. She was not at all in his usual style; in fact, she was positively plain, except for those eyes. No doubt he merely felt obliged to protect her, as he would a sister or a friend.

Unused to probing his sentiments in this way, Gavin crossed to the bell-pull and gave it a vigorous tug. He was engaged to be married. He had already given his mistress her *congé*. He could not afford any such attraction, and therefore it could not exist.

The door opened presently and his valet peered around it enquiringly. "Ask Miss Cherrystone to come down if you would, Metzger." She deserved to know the outcome of his interview with Coombes, and besides, they had yet to trade the results of their separate investigations that day. Idly smoothing his hair with his fingers, Gavin went to seat himself at his desk.

IT WAS WITH SOME trepidation that Frederica answered the summons. She had reached her room only a moment ago and had not yet had time to organize her thoughts in light of Mr. Coombes's unexpected attack. She attempted to do so as she followed Metzger downstairs.

The butler's accusations were preposterous, of course, and obviously not very well thought out. Still, her defence must amount to her word against his, and it seemed only logical that Lord Seabrooke would be more inclined to believe a man who had lived in his household for some time than a female who had resided there merely a week. The only witness she could summon for her conduct was Christabel, and Frederica knew already that she would rather be dismissed than subject the child to Mr. Coombes's evil tongue again. Squaring her shoulders, she walked through the library door when Metzger held it open, ready to meet her fate.

Lord Seabrooke stood at his desk as she entered; there was no one else in the room. "You sent for me, my lord?" She kept her voice as calm as she had during the previous interview, though her senses vibrated at the very sight of the earl, and even more so at the thought of leaving him.

"Yes. Cherry, I wanted you to know at once that Coombes will not trouble you again. He has been dismissed."

Frederica swallowed. "I, ah...thank you, my lord," was all she could think of to say. The ordeal was over, as simply as that! Then she remembered something else Mr. Coombes had said that morning. "Will... will he not seek revenge, though? He knows about Christabel now—"

"It cannot be helped," said the earl. "As I said before, my reputation is scarcely lily white, anyway. This news will not change it appreciably."

Something prompted Frederica to ask, "But what of your recent betrothal? Could such a story not endanger it?" She held her breath, amazed at her own boldness, but anxious to hear his reply.

Lord Seabrooke gave her a twisted smile. "I wondered if you had heard about that. To tell you the truth, I am rather glad you asked. If we are to collaborate in our investigations, there can be no secrets between us, can there?''

Frederica shook her head, though alarm shot through her. Did he suspect? Had he somehow discovered her true identity? His next words reassured her somewhat.

"My betrothal was one of necessity rather than inclination," he said, his blue eyes watching her closely, as if gauging her reaction. "In fact, I have yet to meet my fiancée. I do not even know if she is amenable to the match!"

"Why would you betroth yourself to a lady whom you do not know, my lord?" Frederica kept her tone carefully neutral as she asked a question that had bothered her from the start.

"As I said, necessity. I had fallen deeply in debt after paying off the arrears on my uncle's estate. The income from Brookeside barely covers the cost of upkeep, and with the war over, the army was closed to me. I had even begun to consider fleeing to the Continent. Then Amity died and I found myself with Christabel to consider. A wealthy bride appeared to be the only answer." His eyes begged her to understand, and Frederica felt herself longing to give him the reassurance he sought.

"But what of the lady herself?" she forced herself to ask. "Was she to have no say in the matter?"

"Her brother is her legal guardian," he said shortly, turning away. "It was for him to decide. Of course, I could not force her to wed me were she truly unwilling." He picked up a poker to jab at the fire that already blazed on the hearth. "Now I wonder whether my salvation, and Christabel's, was not too dearly bought. However, though *she* may be able to cry off with honour, I cannot."

"So you are hoping that your fiancée, or her brother, comes to hear of the rumours?" Frederica frowned. "That she will refuse to go through with it?"

The earl sighed. "No, I suppose I cannot hope for that, for it would put me right back where I began. I must hope that when we finally meet, we shall find that we suit. Many a marriage of convenience has eventually become one of affection." His tone was not optimistic.

For the first time, Frederica allowed herself to imagine what it would be like to be married to this man, sharing his name, his home...his bed. The thought created a warm stirring that spread through her midsection. To change the subject, she said quickly, "I finished reading through your sister's letters, my lord."

"Ah! And what did you find?" He, too, seemed eager to abandon the topic of his betrothal.

"There was no direct proof of a marriage, but from Captain Browning's last letter, he plainly intended to visit her shortly and hinted at an elopement. It was also clear that his family wished him to marry another, which may provide a motive for their secrecy."

"What was the date of that letter?" asked the earl. He had replaced the poker in its stand and now leaned on the mantelpiece, looking quite indecently handsome.

Frederica fought to keep her thoughts on the matter at hand. "June of 1810."

The earl raised his brows. "A full year before Christabel's birth. Obviously, he did indeed visit Amity again. We still have nothing to show that they married, however. I fear your theory will have to remain just that, Cherry," he said regretfully.

"I had thought, perhaps, that we might make enquiries across the border. Surely if they were married, even in Scotland, there would be some record of it?"

"You are tenacious, aren't you?" said the earl with a chuckle. "I see little hope in it, but if you wish to write the necessary letters, I will frank them and have them sent off. Christabel is lucky to have such a champion." His gaze lingered on her face, and Frederica felt her colour rise.

"What of your own investigations, my lord?" she asked hurriedly. "Were you able to discover anything about your uncle?"

He shook his head. "Not yet. I asked a few discreet questions, but they may not bear fruit for some time, I fear. I have also requested my man of business to send for the more complete account books. I would be grateful for your assistance when I receive them."

"Certainly, my lord." Again she found herself hoping that some explanation besides treason could be found to account for the disappearance of the Seabrooke fortune. "I can understand why you must proceed slowly with your questioning."

"Yes, even more than Christabel's presence here, a scandal about my uncle's political sympathies would likely sour my upcoming nuptials. Perhaps I should be more forthright in my suspicions." He obviously meant it as a joke, but Frederica thought she caught an underlying seriousness in his voice.

"Pray, do not say that!" she exclaimed. "Not only is your family honour at stake, but perhaps your happiness, as well. You may well find that your betrothed is everything that you would want in a wife."

She knew, suddenly, that she was expressing her own hopes rather than his. "I'll bid you good-night, my lord," she said breathlessly, turning towards the door to avoid his searching regard. "I have letters to write." Before he could reply, she hurried from the library, her heart pounding in her throat at her unexpected discovery. The unimaginable had happened. She had fallen in love with the man she was being forced to marry!

CHAPTER TEN

FOR THE NEXT SEVERAL DAYS, Frederica made it a point to avoid Lord Seabrooke. Until she could untangle her conflicting emotions, it seemed wisest that she keep her distance from him. Letters to the most likely border towns in Scotland were duly written, but rather than handing them to the earl herself, she left them on his desk when she knew he would be out. She also penned a letter to her brother, which she intended to mail from Miss Milliken's house on Thursday to avoid prying eyes. Thomas would be wondering by now why he had not heard from her, and she had no wish for him to come searching for her.

Christabel was growing increasingly fond of her, and that affection was reciprocated. In fact, Frederica found herself frequently falling into the trap of imagining that she would always be there for the child, watching her grow into a young lady she could be proud of. Once or twice she even caught herself musing over what it would be like to sponsor Christabel for her come-out, an experience she herself had shunned. She perceived the danger inherent in such thoughts and strove to suppress them, difficult though it was.

When she visited Miss Milliken on Thursday afternoon, Frederica's former governess greeted her with some disturbing news.

"My dear, I believe it would be best if you left this post as soon as possible," Miss Milliken said as soon as they were seated in the parlour. "Rumours have begun to circulate about Lord Seabrooke. It has become common knowledge that an illegitimate child is in residence, and people are drawing the obvious conclusions."

"Mr. Coombes!" Frederica fairly spat the name. "I suspected that he would do this." Quickly she related the events leading to the butler's dismissal from Seabrooke House.

Miss Milliken nodded in sympathy, but said, "I fear the source of the rumours makes little difference. Once gossip begins to spread, it takes on a life of its own. And there is more."

Frederica looked at her questioningly.

"There has also been some talk about *you,* my dear. Or rather, I should say, about Miss Cherrystone. Her name is being linked with Lord Seabrooke's."

Frederica gasped, not having foreseen that wrinkle. "More of Coombes's malice, I doubt not. What an evil man!"

"Yes, it would appear so. In this case, however, he may have done you a favour. Those two rumours combined may well be enough to persuade your brother to call off your unwanted betrothal to Lord Seabrooke." The woman's warm brown eyes searched Frederica's face. "If it is still unwanted, that is," she added gently.

Frederica sighed. "Oh, Milly, I don't know anymore. Something rather dreadful seems to have happened." She did not notice her friend's sudden stiffening. "Lord Seabrooke and I have somehow become *friends.*"

Miss Milliken relaxed, smiling in her relief. "That doesn't sound so terrible. Is it not what you have wanted in a husband all along?"

"I—I suppose so," said Frederica uncertainly. In truth, she had come to realize that she wished to be far more than a friend to Lord Seabrooke, but she was not ready to admit everything to Milly—not yet.

"I still hate to give Thomas the satisfaction of tamely agreeing to his scheme," she said finally. "I shall continue as Miss Cherrystone for now. Perhaps in that position I can work to silence the rumours. Then, when the time seems right, I shall reveal who I really am."

In vain Miss Milliken sought to dissuade her from this course. "If it becomes known that you have been living in his house all this time, totally unchaperoned, your reputation will be ruined whether you wed him or no," she insisted. "Please, Frederica, do not go back. You may write him a letter from here telling him the truth."

Frederica shook her head. She could think of no more certain way to make him despise her. If she could not have his love, she at least hoped to retain his friendship, and his respect. Besides, as Miss Cherrystone she might be able to discover what his feelings towards her were—and what they could become. "I promise to leave his house before making my public appearance as Miss Chesterton, Milly, if that will make you easier. But I must go back, if only for Christabel's sake."

Miss Milliken gave it up. "Very well, Frederica, though your course of action still seems most unwise to me. To think that it was my idea to place a spy in his household in the first place!"

Frederica gave her counsellor a quick hug. "Everything may yet turn out right, Milly, so do not fret. You must trust that your teachings have taken hold and that I shall be as you would wish: prudent, purposeful—and organized."

GAVIN DIDN'T KNOW whether to be frustrated or relieved. After nearly a week of skilful prying and subtle innuendo, in places ranging from respectable coffee-houses to wretched gaming halls, he was no closer to discovering the late earl's political leanings than he had been at the outset.

He couldn't understand it. From the moment Miss Cherrystone had asked her tentative question, he had been almost certain that his uncle's losses could be traced to the French. The pattern was so exactly what he had seen during his service, when he had investigated just such cases for the War Office. But now, after applying every tactic he had used then, exploring every connection who remained in London, he was beginning to doubt that surmise.

"Thank you, François," he said to the short, dark-haired man who had been his last hope. He had met his erstwhile informant by previous arrangement at an out-of-the-way club well known in certain circles for its political intrigues. "Here is what I promised you." He passed a guinea wrapped in a pound note across the table. "If you hear anything, you know how to contact me."

"Oui, m'sieu," the man answered. "But I cannot think where I should. If your esteemed oncle was a contributor to the Corsican, he was the wiliest one in England. Me, I think you will not need to cover up anything at all."

Gavin had told François that he desired to hide any
trail his uncle had left in view of his impending marriage. François would never have understood that he
might actually wish to expose his uncle's treason, or to
make reparation for it, as far as he was able. And now
it appeared that he would not be able to do so after all.
Gavin was confident that if anyone could have fer-
reted out evidence of Uncle Edmund's French sympathies, it was François.

"Perhaps you are right," he said. "My source may
well have been mistaken."

"Rumours are everywhere, *m'sieu,* but only one in
ten is well founded." François nodded sagely, the ends
of his greasy black moustache bobbing. "If I can be of
service again, you need only call." He tucked the
guinea into his pocket with a cocky smile.

Dressed as he was in a brown furze coat and trou-
sers, Gavin ran little risk from the rougher element as
he walked the half mile to where he had left his carriage. Though François knew his true identity, no one
else was likely to realize that a member of the peerage
was frequenting this unsavoury section of Town.
Glancing quickly about him, he stepped into his carriage, an older one without a crest.

On the way to his solicitor's office, Gavin shrugged
out of his ill-fitting and poorly made clothes and
donned a more respectable ensemble. He waited to tie
his cravat until the carriage had stopped, assuring
himself in the small interior mirror that he looked
much as he always did. A five-month suspension of
practice at such quick changes had not caused his skills
to completely deteriorate, he was pleased to discover.

Still, there were times when a talent for ferreting out
rumours could be decidedly uncomfortable, he

thought. In the course of his search for information about his uncle, certain other gossip had come to his ears that he would far rather not have heard.

As he had feared, Coombes had wasted no time in spreading about Town word of Lord Seabrooke's supposed by-blow. His more disreputable connections had not scrupled to rail him about it, thinking it great fun. That would not have been so bad, as he was prepared to claim Christabel as his own, but there was more. It seemed that Coombes had also sought revenge on Miss Cherrystone by linking her name with his. Some versions of the rumour had Cherry as his live-in mistress, with Christabel their natural child.

The fury Gavin had experienced on first hearing that tale had nearly rivalled what he had felt at Coombes's original accusations. For a moment he wished that he had called the man out at the time, which would have prevented the present assault on Cherry's name. Then the absurdity of his thoughts struck him. What would the world say of an earl who duelled with one of his servants to protect the reputation of another?

The problem was, he could not seem to think of Miss Cherrystone as a servant at all. To be sure, she dressed like one, and was properly deferential when she spoke to him, but there was an intelligence and an unconscious dignity about her that bespoke someone of equal rather than inferior status. He couldn't seem to keep the proper barriers in place between them, at least not in his thoughts.

Gavin had done his best to squelch the gossip, particularly as it related to Cherry, but he knew that he could not stop it altogether. More than ever, he hoped that her theory about Amity's marriage to Peter Browning was sound and could be proved. If he could publicly proclaim Christabel his niece, it would effectively silence both rumours at once.

His man of business was able to inform Gavin that Mr. Trent, the steward he had recently hired to oversee the Seabrooke estate (or what remained of it), would be arriving with the account books that day or the next to go over them with the earl. He had not much hope of gleaning anything useful from them, but it was a place to start, he supposed, as his other lines of investigation had proved fruitless. He would ask Cherry to go over the books with the steward when he arrived; she seemed quite knowledgeable about such things.

On leaving his solicitor's office, Gavin decided to stop by White's for an early dinner before returning home. A respite in such thoroughly respectable surroundings would do him good after the past few days. Never before had he felt so sullied by dealings with London's underworld. Idly, he wondered if it had anything to do with the occasional notion he'd had of what Miss Cherrystone would think if she could see him. The thought made him smile.

Walking into the club, he stopped to take a deep breath, absorbing the almost palpable air of decorum and good breeding that permeated the place. Ignoring the half-dozen dandies at the bow window, whom he might have joined in another mood, he went to sit at a table in a quiet corner. He had not even removed his gloves when he was accosted jovially from behind.

"Seabrooke! Devilish good fortune that I should find you here." Sir Thomas Chesterton clapped him familiarly on the shoulder and seated himself in the other chair. "I've just come from the newspaper offices and wanted to give you fair warning before you were besieged with felicitations.''

The earl favoured his future brother-in-law with a slightly forced smile. ''It is good to see you again, Sir Thomas. Do I take it that you have procured your sister's acquiescence to the match?'' Suddenly he felt as if the walls of a prison were closing about him.

''More or less,'' said Sir Thomas, looking slightly uncomfortable. ''The news took her by surprise, of course, but she's a remarkably levelheaded girl. She can't deny the advantages, and had no reason to expect a better offer.''

Gavin's worst fears were confirmed. The girl was doubtless an antidote, and either brainless or ambitious into the bargain—for what lady of delicacy and intelligence would not revolt at being betrothed sight unseen? ''And when am I to meet my future bride?'' he asked, trying to ignore the sinking feeling in his midsection. He no longer had any appetite.

''Not sure just yet. I *had* hoped to have her in Town by the end of the Little Season.'' Thomas had still to receive a letter from Frederica, and he was beginning to wonder whether he would. He had taken the step of putting the announcement in the papers in hopes of persuading her further that the wedding must take place as planned. Looking at the man across from him, he was somewhat reassured. Seabrooke appeared as solid and dependable as ever; surely Freddie would not be able to find anything to his discredit.

''I say, Seabrooke,'' called out a gentleman entering the club at that moment, whom Thomas was able to identify after a moment as Lord Garvey. ''Haven't seen you in ages.''

Lord Seabrooke rose to shake his hand. "How is wedded bliss treating you, Barry?" he asked. "Are you in Town for long?"

Garvey shook his head. "Only for a few weeks. Elizabeth wants our first child to be born in the country." He was grinning with pride. "My heir is due to make his appearance before Christmas. Speaking of offspring, that reminds me. I heard a most unlikely on-dit this very day," he said, sobering somewhat.

"Don't put much stock in tittle-tattle," said Lord Seabrooke hastily. "I have it on good authority that only one rumour in ten is well founded. Tell me, have you met Sir Thomas Chesterton?"

Garvey had, but he allowed the previous subject to drop while he renewed his acquaintance with the young man. After a few minutes of general conversation, Lord Garvey was called away to answer someone's enquiries about the Duke of Ravenham, whose estate neighboured his own. When he had gone, Seabrooke turned back to his young companion.

"Have you dined yet, Sir Thomas?" he asked. White's was becoming crowded and he feared that some of his other friends might have heard the same gossip Garvey had and require him to confirm or deny it.

"No, I haven't," Sir Thomas replied.

"I've engaged an excellent cook at Seabrooke House. What do you say to joining me?" If Sir Thomas had to learn of Christabel's existence, Gavin preferred to acquaint him with the facts himself, privately. If Chesterton were thoroughly appalled, there might still be time to retract the betrothal announcement before it appeared in the papers on the morrow.

THOUGH SHE HAD done her best to reassure Miss Milliken, Frederica felt far from confident that she would be able to find a solution to the muddle she had created. So many new problems had arisen since she had finally rejected her plan of proving Lord Seabrooke a rogue. Now she had to resolve the question of Christabel's legitimacy, the mystery of the Seabrooke fortune, and, most of all, the riddle of the earl's feelings towards herself—and towards his betrothal. She had no more wish to force him into a loveless match than she had to be forced into one herself. It was imperative that she discover his wishes on the matter.

These thoughts served to while away the hackney ride back to Seabrooke House, but once there she felt no closer to a plan of action. Christabel was happy to see her, exclaiming over the hair ribands she had brought back as a gift and demanding to try them on at once. Frederica willingly complied, submerging all thoughts of her absurd situation in the soothing familiarity of the nursery and her routine here. Once Christabel was settled for the night, however, the thoughts came surging back and she made a sudden decision.

She would never advance the resolution of any of her problems if she spent all her time hidden away in the nursery. It was time she moved forward on all fronts, and the only way to do that was to confront Lord Seabrooke face to face. They had not consulted over their separate investigations since Saturday evening; surely he would not think it odd if she were to come to the library again after dinner to ask what progress had been made. Sternly refusing to acknowledge the trembling in her stomach, Frederica tidied her wig, touched up her freckles, straightened her glasses and went downstairs.

On the first-floor landing, she paused. Were there voices coming from the dining-room? It had not occurred to her that the earl might have company. He frequently dined out, but she could not recall him inviting anyone to the house for dinner since she had been here. Perhaps he was merely speaking to the footman, Jeffries, who had taken over Mr. Coombes's duties until another butler could be hired.

Frederica decided to wait in the library. If Lord Seabrooke did have guests, they would doubtless go to the parlour after dinner, and she could simply return to the nursery. And if they did by chance come to the library, she could pretend to be looking for a book. Accordingly, when she heard the dining-room doors open, she positioned herself near one of the shelves, pretending to scan the titles. Yes, there was another male voice besides the earl's, and it was certainly not Jeffries's. In fact, it sounded remarkably like...

To Frederica's horror, the handle of the library door began to turn. In desperation, she dived behind a large chair in the corner, one that was seldom used, and crouched there, holding her breath. Lord Seabrooke and his guest entered the library and seated themselves near the fire on the opposite side of the room. Peering cautiously around the edge of her chair, Frederica was relieved to see that both men had their backs to her. Even so, there was no mistaking that handsome blond profile when the earl's guest turned to speak. It was Thomas!

Of all the people in England, why did he have to invite my brother to dinner? Frederica wondered frantically. *And what am I to do now?*

Of course, all she *could* do was remain hidden. Revealing herself now was completely out of the question, for there was no knowing what Thomas might do or say were he to recognize her. As her heart slowed its fevered pounding, thought became possible again and the answer to her first question also came clear. Thomas was doubtless here to discuss her betrothal. What could be more natural than for him to call on his future brother-in-law upon his return to London?

At that thought, some of her original resentment at his insolent handling of her future returned. Could he not at least have waited until he heard from her before coming to Town to solidify his plans? The letter she has posted that afternoon would not reach him now, of course. She would have to discover his lodgings and write to him there. Her courage bolstered by irritation, she began to listen to their conversation, which they had apparently begun during dinner.

"In fact," Thomas was saying, "I'm beginning to think losing that twelve thousand pounds to you was the best thing I could have done. Otherwise Freddie might well have remained unwed to her dying day."

"And you don't foresee any problems when she hears about the child?" asked the earl.

Frederica's mind barely registered the fact that Lord Seabrooke had revealed Christabel's existence to her brother. Her whole attention was focussed instead on what Thomas had just said. Did that mean that her betrothal had been the result of a *wager*? Her face burned at the thought.

"No, no," Thomas answered expansively, making Frederica suspect that he had been drinking rather heavily. "Freddie loves children. Besides, five years is a long—" He was interrupted by a tap at the library door.

The earl rose to open it, and Frederica heard the footman say, "A Mr. Trent to see you, m'lord. I've put him in the front parlour."

"Very well, Jeffries. Ask Mrs. Abbott to prepare a room for him. He will be staying for a day or two. Sir Thomas—" he turned back to his guest "—pray help yourself to another glass. I shall return in a few moments." He followed Jeffries out of the room.

Frederica did not stop to think, so outraged was she over what she had heard a moment before. The instant the door closed behind Lord Seabrooke, she sprang from her hiding place to confront her brother.

He turned at the sound of her step and blinked, plainly wondering how she had materialized in the middle of the room. "Lord Seabrooke is in the parlour, ma'am," he said politely, though he frowned in confusion. "Are you Mrs. Abbott? I believe he has instructions for you."

"No, I am not Mrs. Abbott," said Frederica clearly, and had the satisfaction of seeing Thomas's jaw drop at the sound of her voice. "Thomas, I believe we have something to discuss."

CHAPTER ELEVEN

"FREDDIE?" Sir Thomas gaped at his sister in disbelief. "What the devil are you doing here? And in that get-up?"

"Never mind that for the moment. I would have an explanation from you first. Did I understand you to say that my betrothal to Lord Seabrooke was to pay off a *gambling debt* of yours? How *dared* you do such a thing?" Though she kept her voice low, it shook with fury.

Thomas pulled his fascinated gaze from her face with a visible effort and examined the toes of his polished Hessians. After a lengthy pause, he sighed. "Yes, Freddie, I lost heavily at cards to Seabrooke last month. As my money is all tied up in that blasted trust," he said bitterly, "I had no way to make good on the debt at once. Your name came up in conversation, and once I had told him about you, he seemed quite eager for the match. I—I didn't tell you, because I knew you'd kick up the devil of a fuss, just as you are doing now." He met her eyes again with a frown. "But that don't explain what *you* are doing here! How did you manage to sneak into Seabrooke House?" He glanced over at the fastened window casements.

"I came to discover more about him so that I could hold you to your agreement," she snapped. "Milly helped me to get a position as Christabel's nanny." She decided there was no point in telling him about that first interview, and her suspicions at the time.

Thomas's expression became thunderous. "Do you mean to say that you've actually been living under the man's roof? For how long?"

"About ten days now, but—"

"And you have the audacity to take *me* to task?" He was now fully as angry as she. "You realize, of course, that your reputation is completely ruined?"

"Ssh! Moderate your tone, Thomas. Lord Seabrooke has no notion of whom I am, as yet, and I would prefer to keep it that way," hissed Frederica, with a hasty glance towards the door. "As long as no one discovers that Miss Cherrystone and Miss Chesterton are one and the same, my reputation should not suffer. And how can you presume to condemn me when it was you who forced me into this situation to begin with?"

Brother and sister glared at each other for a long moment, and in the sudden silence, they heard firm footsteps coming toward the library. Frederica said quickly, "Meet me in Hyde Park tomorrow morning. We can discuss it further there."

The door opened, and she turned. "Good evening, my lord," she said smoothly. "I came to find a book. I had no notion that you were entertaining this evening."

Lord Seabrooke raised his eyebrows slightly at the sight of the nanny face to face with his future brother-in-law, but he merely said, "I take it you have made the acquaintance of Sir Thomas Chesterton?"

Thomas remained mute, apparently still struggling with the remarkable situation, so Frederica said quickly, "I've only been here a moment, my lord. I fear I rather startled Sir Thomas."

"Then allow me to present Christabel's nanny, Miss Cherrystone. Cherry has made herself most invaluable to us already," he added, with a warm smile at Frederica.

She returned it perfunctorily, fearful of what Thomas might think. "Pleased to meet you, sir," she said, bobbing a quick curtsey. "I'll just get my book and leave you gentlemen to your brandy. My apologies for intruding."

Seizing a volume at random, she hurried from the room before she could lose her precarious control. Once in the hallway, the door safely closed behind her, she had to fight an incredible urge to giggle. What an absurd situation! Glancing down, she noticed the title of the book she held. *A Thesis on Geometrical Equations*. One hand over her mouth, she ran for the stairs before her laughter could bring the earl or the servants to investigate.

Gavin, meanwhile, watched her go with something like regret. Why had he not informed her that Sir Thomas was his future brother-in-law? The more unavoidable his approaching wedding became, the more he felt, with every fibre of his being, that he was doing the wrong thing.

ON THE WAY to the Park the next morning, Frederica wondered whether she ought to give Christabel some warning about their meeting with her brother. Glancing down at the child's happy, shining face, she decided against it. They had brought along another sack of stale bread to feed to the ducks, and her charge would doubtless be too occupied with that favourite pastime to notice whom her nanny spoke to.

Thomas was awaiting them at the Park gates.

"Good morning, Sir Thomas," she said with a polite nod. "How pleasant to see you here. Would you care to walk with us to the duck pond?"

He took his cue from her and answered in the same style, and they conversed on general topics until Christabel was surrounded by an eager flock of ducks and laughing happily as she fed them.

"Now, perhaps you will explain to me what is going on," Thomas said softly once they had moved a short distance away. "I nearly had an apoplexy when I saw you at Seabrooke House last night. Why are you not at Miss Milliken's?"

"I was," replied Frederica. "It became obvious that the only way I could discover anything of importance about Lord Seabrooke was by becoming a spy in his household." She went on to describe the procedure they had followed to procure her position there.

Thomas listened with open scepticism. "And has it worked? Have you managed to prove him a scoundrel?"

Frederica bit her lip. It rankled to admit to Thomas that he had been right, but the only alternative was to ruin a man she now considered a good friend. "He is no saint, that is certain," she said finally. "But no, I cannot call him a scoundrel. Though I still think it reprehensible of you to betroth me to him without my consent!" Her green eyes met his blue ones squarely. "It was hardly likely to promote a felicitous marriage. And now I fear that may be even harder to achieve. He is far from happy about the match himself, Thomas."

"He gave no hint of that to me," her brother protested. "Not even when I informed him that I had put the announcement in the papers yesterday."

"How dared you do so when I had not finished my investigation?" Frederica flared. "You could not know that I would not find anything!"

Thomas looked smug. "But you have not, have you? And it is just as well, for I'd never let you off marrying him now that you've been living in the same house with him! We can only hope that word of it never leaks out. Still," he said, looking at her with respect, "it was a plucky thing to do, Freddie, and more than I expected of you."

"It is good in you to say so," she said cuttingly. "But I have another concern. How am I to reveal what I have done? Lord Seabrooke does not strike me as a man who will look kindly on deceit."

"Perhaps you need not tell him. Quit your post as nanny and appear as yourself. He may never make the connection."

Frederica cast him a withering glance. "I'll grant that *you* might be fooled, Thomas, but Lord Seabrooke is more observant. He'll know who I am the moment I speak two words to him. I don't believe he is the sort of man who puts great stock in appearances." She wondered if that were wishful thinking on her part. Still, if she could win his affection as plain Miss Cherrystone, she would have proof positive that he did not care merely for her fortune or her beauty. Then she would wed him most willingly—if he would still have her!

"Give me just a few more days," she said. She could not reasonably delay longer than that; the Little Season was already begun. "Make the arrangements for my official arrival in Town. I'll make out a list of what you must do." Already she was mentally arranging things. "You must take a house in Mayfair, send for my wardrobe.... I shall send you a note detailing everything. In less than a fortnight, if all goes well, Miss Frederica Chesterton will make her formal debut!"

WHEN FREDERICA RETURNED to Seabrooke House, she found Lucy hovering near the back entrance, waiting for her. "His lordship wishes to see you in the library at your earliest convenience, miss," she said, her eyes alight with curiosity. "I'll stay with Miss Christabel until you return."

Thanking her, Frederica hurried through the house. Lord Seabrooke greeted her with a smile that made her realize fully how much she had missed his company during the past few days.

"Cherry!" he greeted her jovially, making her wonder giddily if the feeling were mutual. "I've received a letter from an innkeeper in Coldstream. It appears your hypothesis was well founded. In his marriage book, he has a record of a wedding, over the anvil, of a Miss Amity Alexander and a Captain Peter Browning!" He waved the letter at her delightedly.

"Oh, my lord, that is all that is wonderful!" cried Frederica, other considerations forgotten in her happiness for Christabel. "Now you can openly declare Christabel your niece!"

"And we owe it all to you, Cherry," exclaimed the earl, coming forward to clasp her in a hug much like the ones he was wont to give Christabel. "Thank you."

Even as Frederica returned his embrace without thinking, he amazed her by kissing her full on the mouth. Overcome by the excitement of the moment, she returned the kiss in the same spirit, only to be betrayed by the intensity of her own feelings. His clasp tightened and her arms slid up his back, almost of their own volition. Imperceptibly, what had been a congratulatory kiss became something else entirely.

As he deepened the kiss, Frederica's mind spun, an incredible surge of desire sweeping over her. *What on earth was she doing?* Though being in his arms felt much, much more wonderful than she had even imagined, she stiffened in spite of herself. He released her at once, looking acutely embarrassed. For herself, she was certain her face was flaming.

"I, ah, suppose you will wish to tell the staff first, my lord," she stammered, not meeting his eyes.

"Yes, I'll let Mrs. Abbott handle that. She'll be delighted, I doubt not." He seemed exceedingly interested in a porcelain figurine on the mantelpiece. "Could you ask her to step in here when you go?"

"Certainly, my lord." Frederica turned toward the door. The ebbing storm of emotion both elated and confused her. Had he felt something as well, or had she merely imagined the look in his eyes?

"Oh, I almost forgot," he said, halting her. "My steward arrived from Brookeside last night with the quarterly account books. Would you mind terribly going over them with me, ah . . . with him, this afternoon or perhaps tomorrow?"

"Of course not, my lord." Their glances met for an instant and her heart began to race again.

"Thank you, Cherry," said the earl again, and she knew he did not only refer to her willingness to look over the books.

With a quick nod, Frederica vacated the room to go in search of Mrs. Abbott.

To avoid dwelling on the scene just past, and the feelings it had unexpectedly aroused in him, Gavin forced himself to concentrate on his interview with Mrs. Abbott, who appeared after a mercifully short interval.

"So you see, it would doubtless be best if we were to act as though we always knew Christabel to be Amity's legitimate daughter," he said, after explaining to her what he and Cherry had discovered, and how. He had made no secret of the fact that Miss Cherrystone deserved the bulk of the credit for salvaging his sister's reputation and Christabel's future.

Mrs. Abbott nodded at the conclusion. "I've always discouraged the staff from speculating about her anyways, m'lord—them what knew about her at all, that is. 'Twon't be the work of a day to convince them that I knew about this all along, and that you was just waiting until she was settled in before letting on she was here. I'll say she's been a bit poorly—that'll be explanation enough."

"Excellent! I knew I could rely on you to handle the matter, Mrs. Abbott." Gavin smiled broadly at her, glad to have the matter so easily taken care of. If anyone asked him about Coombes's story now, he could simply dismiss it as the tale of a disgruntled servant he had fired for just cause.

"And what about Miss Cherry?" asked the housekeeper abruptly, breaking into his satisfying thoughts.

"What about her?"

"You know as well as I, m'lord, that she's not a proper person to be the nanny of an earl's legitimate niece. Don't forget that I'm the one who checked out her references. Most of them were false."

"Yes, yes, I know." In truth, Gavin had tried to forget the fact, and had nearly succeeded. "But surely she has proved that she is capable of the post. Look at what she has done for Christabel! And they are quite attached to each other, you know."

Mrs. Abbott nodded sagely. "That they are. I was thinking more about what others would have to say about her. Of course, there's another post available that doesn't require such demanding references," she said with a knowing smile as she headed for the door.

"Another post?" Gavin had no idea what she was talking about. "What post is that?"

"Countess," said Mrs. Abbott succinctly, and let herself out of the library.

Gavin gaped at the closed library door. Now what on earth had she meant by that? He had known the old housekeeper had not entirely approved of his keeping Miss Cherrystone on after discovering that her references were false, and he had assumed that she did not care much for the girl as a result. It appeared that he had been wrong.

As far as he could recall, Mrs. Abbott had never before given him personal advice. She had known Gavin from birth, of course, and he knew that she regarded him almost as a son, which made it that much harder to discount her words now.

Did she actually mean that she thought he should marry Cherry instead of his heiress? Oddly enough, the idea rather appealed to him once he allowed himself to consider it. Though she could have no fortune, Cherry was exactly what would suit him in a wife: intelligent and kind, with none of the airs and graces that were so prevalent among fashionable debutantes. She was certainly not grasping or ambitious, as he had reason to believe his betrothed might be, and the better he came to know her, the lovelier she appeared to him.

Gavin turned back to his desk with an oath. What could it matter if Cherry were the perfect woman for him and if he should be madly in love with her? He was legally and morally bound to marry Miss Frederica Chesterton, and there was no way that he could, in honour, change that.

Though he rarely imbibed before dinner, Gavin decided that he needed a drink. Crossing to the sideboard, he poured himself a generous measure of brandy.

GAVIN WAS FEELING considerably more mellow, though he was by no means bosky, when Sir Thomas Chesterton came to call on him an hour later. His guest's first words were sufficient to dispel the comfortable glow the spirits had induced.

"Glad I found you in, Seabrooke," he said, breezing in to seat himself in the chair before the desk. "I got word from my sister today that she'll be coming to Town for the end of the Little Season after all. She should arrive in a week or so, and make her bow shortly after that. I'll be handling all the arrangements at this end, and have agreed to see a house over on Audley Square this afternoon, so I'll have to miss our session at Gentleman Jackson's. I believe she's eager to meet you."

"Is she indeed?" asked Gavin, trying to ignore a feeling of impending doom. "Suppose she doesn't care for what she sees?"

"Not likely," said Sir Thomas with a laugh. "Anyway, she had her chance to cry off and didn't take it. Don't you worry, I shan't let her cut up stiff now."

Gavin had come to realize that Sir Thomas was going to be more than a little relieved to see his sister safely married. The girl must be a harpy as well as an antidote! Now she was to be his wife, and there was nothing he could do about it. Taking a gulp of brandy to fortify himself, he turned to Sir Thomas.

"Why don't why have bit of a celebration here tomorrow night to mark my betrothal to your sister? One last hurrah, as it were, before I don the mantle of sober respectability. You can meet some of my closest acquaintances, and it will give them a chance to offer their congratulations *en masse*." If Lord Seabrooke's smile held a hint of desperation, Sir Thomas did not appear to notice.

CHAPTER TWELVE

FREDERICA SPENT the remainder of the day happily making some of the changes appropriate to Christabel's new status. Mrs. Abbott had informed her that the earl had allotted a considerable sum to be spent on the nursery and his niece, but there had been no opportunity before to spend it. As there was no longer any need for secrecy, Frederica was now able to remedy that. She and Christabel spent an enjoyable afternoon shopping for toys, books and clothes to fill the previous lack.

When they returned, well past Christabel's usual nap time, they were both laden with purchases, and Christabel was clad in a crisp new frock of sky blue that matched her eyes, with a snowy-white pinafore in place of the stained and patched one she had worn when they left. Out of habit, Frederica began to head around to the back entrance, then stopped with a laugh.

"We'll go in through the front door for a change, shall we, darling?"

Christabel agreed readily, not understanding the symbolic difference between the two entrances. To Frederica, however, this was a declaration of Christabel's elevated status. Proudly she marched her charge up the broad marble steps and through the grand portico of Seabrooke House, as she now had every right to do.

As they passed the library, Frederica suddenly remembered that the earl had asked her to examine the estate records with his steward. She paused outside the door, wondering whether she should stop to apologize for her absence. But before she could knock, she heard masculine voices, raised uproariously in song. One was the earl's, and the other, quite definitely, belonged to her brother. Wondering that they should be foxed, as they evidently were, so early in the evening, she hurried Christabel on past the library to the stairs. It appeared that the books would not be attended to that day.

Back in the nursery, she and Christabel spent the remaining time until supper unwrapping their purchases and arranging them about the nursery and in the clothes-press. Frederica reflected that even if she were to leave tomorrow and never see Christabel or her uncle again, she had done far too much good here to regret her stay. The thought of leaving, however, came with a pang that no amount of self-recrimination would allay.

"Is it not grand, Cherry, that the sick lady next door has moved away?" asked Christabel. That was the reason Frederica had given her to account for the sudden changes taking place. "Now I can go into the garden any time I like and not worry about the noise I make."

"You certainly may, dear," Frederica assured her. "And I have another thought. Would you like to have a peacock in the garden? I have one that I can fetch, for your uncle said that I might bring you any pets I wished to."

"A peacock?" Christabel was entranced at the thought. "Will he spread his feathers for me?"

"I'm certain we can induce him to do so," replied Frederica with a laugh. "Perhaps, if Lucy will come up to the nursery after your supper, I can go to get him this very evening."

"That would be wonderful, Cherry!" Christabel interrupted her own effusions with a yawn, reminding Frederica that the child had missed her customary nap.

"I'll run down to get your supper and ask her. I think you could use an early night, young lady!" She returned Christabel's impulsive hug with misty eyes and hurried down to the kitchens, trying not to think about the parting that must come so soon.

At her query, Mrs. Abbott informed her that Lord Seabrooke had gone out. The disapproval on her face told Frederica that his intoxication had not escaped her notice, either. Nevertheless, she had no fault to find with Frederica's plan, so long as she was back early. Promising to be gone no more than an hour or two, Frederica left.

MISS MILLIKEN was pleased, if startled, to see Frederica again so soon. "So you have taken my advice!" she exclaimed. "Good. I could not be happy about your situation at Seabrooke House, with all the gossip flying about Town."

"The chatter is no longer of consequence, Milly," Frederica informed her with a smile. "Lord Seabrooke received a letter today proving that Christabel's parents were legally wed. He can now openly claim her as his niece—his *legitimate* niece—without besmirching his sister's name. Christabel can now have the life she deserves, rather than the one you predicted for her." She could not prevent a trace of smugness from creeping into her voice.

"I am very happy for the child, truly," Miss Milliken assured her, "but there is still the matter of your name being linked with Lord Seabrooke's. How long can you keep up this charade, Frederica?"

"The news about Christabel, once it becomes known, should effectively silence the other rumours as well, I should think," she replied. "As to your query, I cannot remain there as Miss Cherrystone much longer. Thomas is in Town."

She related the scene in the library the night before, as well as her subsequent conversation with her brother in the Park that morning. Miss Milliken listened attentively, torn between horror and laughter.

"What a shock that must have been for him!" she finally said with a chuckle. "Perhaps being on the receiving end of a prank for a change will do him some good. But he is right." She sobered. "You have had your chance to discredit Lord Seabrooke and have failed. A wise general knows when to signal retreat; it is only fair that you now honour the betrothal."

Frederica sighed. "Fair of me, perhaps, but is it fair to Lord Seabrooke? He agreed to the betrothal out of necessity, but I believe he is far from happy about it. And now I suspect that he may be beginning to care for Miss Cherrystone, at least as a friend."

"If you are not careful, Frederica, you will end up being jealous of yourself," Miss Milliken chided her. "You must reveal the truth to him eventually. Why wait longer?"

As she had with Thomas that morning, Frederica temporized. "I have a few days yet before I must begin preparing for my debut. You will act as my chaperone, will you not, Milly?" Her companion nodded, but her eyes still held a question.

"I'll find a way to tell him before then, I'm certain," Frederica said firmly, trying to convince herself, as well.

Miss Milliken continued to regard her severely, but Frederica quickly stood. "I promised to be back within the hour, and I have yet to collect Fanfare. Do help me get him into his cage, won't you?" She still had not the slightest idea how she was to disclose her deception to the earl, and her thoughts instinctively shied away from the possible consequences.

Taking refuge in action, she hurried out to Milly's small garden to collect the peacock and made a great fuss over loading the cage into the hackney for the return journey. The driver made no little fuss about the matter himself, and Frederica was fully occupied in soothing first him, then the affronted bird during the trip to Seabrooke House. The matter of her charade would have to wait, at least until the morrow.

THE NEXT MORNING, Christabel was up at first light, eager to see the peacock. After a hurried breakfast, she accompanied Frederica down to the garden—openly, for the first time.

"Here, Christabel, throw a bit of grain onto the ground and Fanfare will come right to you. He's very tame," said Frederica, giving the child a handful of the feed she had brought along. Soon the peacock was eating at their feet.

"He's so beautiful, Cherry," said Christabel in an awed whisper, stroking the iridescent neck.

"Yes, he certainly is," agreed Lord Seabrooke from the top of the steps leading into the garden. "Where on earth did he come from?"

Frederica whirled at the sound of his voice, causing
the peacock to startle, but Christabel answered at once.

"Cherry brought him for me to play with, Uncle
Gavin! She says his name is Fanfare." She gave Frederica one of her impulsive hugs. "I just love Cherry,
don't you?"

Frederica knew that she had flushed scarlet at the
child's innocent question and quickly turned back to
the bird to hide her face. The earl, meanwhile, was
making a great business of clearing his throat.

"Cherry has certainly been a valuable addition to the
household," he finally said rather stiffly. "I am curious, however, where she managed to find a peacock
here in the city."

Stung by his dry tone, in which Frederica thought she
detected an accusation, she dared to meet his gaze with
a challenging one of her own. "He is mine, my lord. A
friend was keeping him for me. You did say that I
might bring any pets here that I wished." Her own
voice was sharp.

Lord Seabrooke's face relaxed, and she realized that
she had misinterpreted. "Yes, I did," he replied easily, "and I've no objection to his being here, provided
he does not indulge in that infernal screeching they are
prone to. I did not realize you had pets even more ex-
otic than mice, Cherry." His look was both teasing
and, oddly, entreating.

For one breathless moment, Frederica was tempted
to pour out the whole story to him, to tell him who she
really was and why she was here. He seemed to sense
something of her struggle, for the plea in his eyes grew
more pronounced. Mercifully, she recalled Christabel's presence in time. "I had Angora goats at one time

as well, my lord," she said at last. "But they are not now in Town."

"I must be grateful for that, I suppose." Although his words and tone were still light, there was something of withdrawal in his expression. Frederica, her eyes still locked with his, perceived the fact and guessed its cause. She would *have* to tell him soon!

"Uncle Gavin, do you want to pet him?" asked Christabel, giving both Frederica and the earl an excuse to break that too intimate gaze.

"Perhaps later, Christabel. I came out here to ask Miss Cherrystone if she could find the time this morning to go over the books with Mr. Trent." His manner was suddenly formal. "Ralph, here, can keep an eye on you and your new friend." He nodded behind them to a lad who had just come into the garden through the gate from the mews.

Ralph, who came two mornings a week to tend the garden, had stopped to stare at the peacock, but on hearing his name, he eagerly pulled on his straw-coloured forelock. "Yes, yer lordship! I'll watch 'em like a hawk!" he fervently agreed.

"Excellent. I've no doubt my niece will be well looked after," said the earl.

Frederica saw the speculative twinkle in the boy's eyes and realized that Lord Seabrooke had chosen his words carefully. Word of Christabel's relationship to him would doubtless begin to spread about Town that very morning, countering Mr. Coombes's vicious rumours. She gave Christabel and Ralph the remainder of the grain and followed the earl indoors.

"Mr. Trent is already in the library," he said to her as they passed into the front hallway. "I am planning an impromptu entertainment tonight, and have several calls to make, but I hope to join you later on. Feel free to spend as long as is necessary on the books. Mrs. Abbott or one of the maids can take your place with Christabel for the day."

His tone was still formal, as though he were holding himself rigidly in check. Frederica looked up at him questioningly, her lips slightly parted while she tried to frame the words she knew she must speak. To her amazement, she saw something like a shudder ran through him and then he turned away abruptly.

"I'll bid you good-morning then," he said almost roughly, and strode towards the front door before she could reply.

Frederica watched him go, blinking in surprise at his odd change of manner. He must have been preoccupied with his plans for the evening, she decided. With a shrug, she opened the library door, hoping that she and the steward might find something that would enable her to preface her revelation with good news.

GAVIN WALKED quickly away from Seabrooke House, his thoughts and feelings in turmoil. Why in blazes had Mrs. Abbott put that idea into his head yesterday? Since his interview with the housekeeper, he had scarcely been able to think of anything but Cherry. He had concocted this evening's assembly in hopes of distracting himself, but so far it had not worked. Even the brandy he had drunk the previous night had done nothing but break down his last reservations, finally allowing him to admit to himself the very feeling he was trying so hard now to deny.

He was in love with Christabel's nanny. There it was: the plain, unvarnished truth. He had hoped that in the cold light of day he would be able to dismiss that remarkable discovery as an alcohol-induced fantasy, but if anything, his conviction remained stronger than ever. Never having been in love before, he could attribute the powerful emotions that assailed him to no other cause.

By thunder, when she had looked up at him outside the library door just now, it had taken every ounce of his control not to kiss her right there, in the front hall! What would she have done if he had? he wondered. Probably slapped him across the face and given notice, he thought ruefully. And rightly so. He had no business indulging in such fancies about a servant, even such an unusual one as Cherry. Especially when he would be meeting his promised wife within two weeks!

Forcing his thoughts to the evening ahead out of pure self-defence, Gavin directed his steps towards Lord Jocelyn's house to deliver his first invitation.

MR. TRENT was an earnest, ambitious man, but Frederica soon realized that the steward was not particularly clever. He was competent enough, she supposed, to be trusted with the running of an estate diminished to the current size of Brookeside, but she would have been reluctant to allow him the management of Maple Hill.

"Did you ever think to cross-check the different account books?" she asked him in exasperation after nearly an hour's work had revealed further puzzles, rather than answers.

The steward ran a hand through his thinning brown hair and regarded her nervously. His attitude towards her had changed dramatically over the past hour, from amused condescension to blustering defensiveness and, finally, to grudging respect.

"Don't forget, miss, that I've only had the running of Brookeside and the other Seabrooke holdings for a few months. There was no steward at all for the past year and more—seems the old earl kept the books himself after Mr. Collins retired."

Frederica strove for patience. "Yes, you've told me so already. But in those months, did you do nothing to verify his totals?"

Mr. Trent blinked owlishly at her. "No one ever told me to do so. I did make certain that income exceeded expenditures, and the picture has improved considerably since I came aboard, as you can surely see!"

"You've done an admirable job at that, certainly," said Frederica soothingly, realizing that she had pricked his pride yet again. "And of course you had no way of knowing that Lord Seabrooke would ask for this sort of investigation into his uncle's finances." She sighed. The quarterly books had merely echoed the ledger: money had been bled from the estate for unknown reasons, beginning three years ago and continuing almost to the time of the previous earl's death. "May I see those other papers you brought?"

"Ah, now here you'll find I've done a bit of investigating after all," said Mr. Trent proudly, digging into his satchel. He beamed at her as he handed them across the desk. "When word came from Mr. Culpepper a week ago, I did some exploring and found that the old earl had more than just the one strongbox in his study. He also had a safe of sorts in his bedchamber." His smile faded. "But it contained only these deeds, no money. And they aren't even for the land around Brookeside."

Frederica examined the documents curiously. "No, you are right, they are from another county entirely—

Cornwall, in fact. Nor do they represent a great deal of
land, for all he apparently paid for them." She looked
at them carefully, noting the dates of purchase. "This
is certainly where the money went, however, for the
first purchase coincides with the time he began mort-
gaging the Seabrooke lands. Hmm." She pondered for
a moment, then glanced back at the ledger. An investment had been noted on that date. In sudden excitement, she asked, "Have we any way of knowing what
this land is now worth?"

Mr. Trent looked perplexed. "I suppose Mr. Culpepper, his lordship's man of business, could find
out," he said uncertainly.

"Take these to him at once, Mr. Trent! I believe we
may well have solved Lord Seabrooke's riddle—and
perhaps his financial difficulties, as well!"

BY EARLY AFTERNOON, Lord Seabrooke had secured
the acceptance of nearly two dozen people, all among
the more unconventional members of the ton, to attend his spur-of-the-moment rout. It was to be an in-
formal affair, and he had advised everyone that they
were free to spread word of it to whoever they might
encounter. While he could not expect a crush, his assembly should be well attended, he thought with satisfaction. He needed the distraction.

The flood of congratulations and well wishes he received in the course of his calls had done little to dispel his unease over his inappropriate feelings towards
Miss Cherrystone. If anything, his doubts had been
increased.

Gavin wished he had a confidant, someone who
might advise him about the matter. He now realized, as
though for the first time, that although he had numer-

ous acquaintances whose company he enjoyed, he had no really close friends. He supposed his years as a soldier, and later as a spy of sorts, must account for it. Odd that he had never noticed it before. Mentally cataloguing everyone he knew, he was forced to admit that the only person he felt comfortable confiding in was Cherry—and she would obviously not do in this case!

Still, he had been reminded in the course of his visits that numerous of his acquaintances had made marriages of convenience and scraped along quite comfortably. Surely he could do so as well? In fact, as he headed back to Seabrooke House, he almost managed to convince himself that he was doing the only possible thing in marrying an heiress. It was what Society expected, and it would allow him and, more importantly, Christabel (whom he had casually mentioned during nearly every call) to move in the convivial circle he currently enjoyed. If Miss Chesterton was not a complete crosspatch, perhaps she would come to enjoy it, too.

It was in this precariously settled frame of mind that he entered the house and went at once to the library. There he found Mr. Trent awaiting him. He should be grateful, he supposed, that Cherry had already returned to the nursery; ruthlessly, he ignored the pang of disappointment he felt at her absence. Only then did he notice that his steward was smiling broadly.

"Praise be you're back, my lord, for I've been fair bursting to tell you the good news," he exclaimed at once. "Of course, it was Miss Cherrystone's idea to check out those deeds—an exceptional young woman, my lord, I must say."

Gavin nodded in complete agreement with that sentiment before prodding the man to continue. "Deeds?"

"Yes, my lord. I didn't think much of them, but Miss Cherrystone, she figured out what they were right away. I took them to Mr. Culpepper, as she suggested, and he was able to trace them in under an hour. He wishes to acquaint you with the details himself, but it seems your uncle bought some old copper mines in Cornwall that have begun producing again over the past year or so. He died before the profits came in, and as he bought them through an agent, there was some confusion over who the owner was. You are a very wealthy man, my lord!"

CHAPTER THIRTEEN

FREDERICA REACHED the foot of the stairs just in time to hear Mr. Trent's last words and almost cursed to herself. She had so wanted to be the one to tell Lord Seabrooke the good news! Why had he returned just then, when she had run up to the nursery to check on Christabel and to tidy her mousy wig? She was tempted to flee back up the stairs, but before she could do so, the earl turned and saw her.

"It seems I owe you yet another debt of gratitude, Cherry," he said, coming forward. "I'll have to see if I can find any other problems for you to solve for me!"

She retreated a step, fearing a repetition of yesterday's hug. Her heart was pounding so, she would never manage to maintain her composure were he to embrace her again! "I—I am happy to be of service, my lord," she said breathlessly.

To her relief, Lord Seabrooke made no move to touch her. Still grinning, he said, "At the very least, you must receive a substantial bonus for this morning's work. I shall go at once to Culpepper's office to learn all the particulars, and I'll inform you of them when I return. Will you come to the library this evening?" Something in his expression told her that he was recalling the other occasions when they had met there.

"I thought you were expecting guests tonight," she said quickly, very much aware of Mr. Trent's interest in their conversation. The man might not be clever, but he was no fool, either. The last thing she needed was another spate of gossip!

The earl smacked his forehead with one hand. "So I am! And now I really do have something to celebrate. Which reminds me, I have told all of my acquaintance about my niece, who is *newly* come to live with me." He gave her a significant look. "I should like to introduce her to them tonight, if you will consent to bring her down. Will you, Miss Cherrystone?"

Frederica realized with a start that the gathering must have originally been planned as a sort of betrothal party—and that Lord Seabrooke saw that event as nothing worthy of celebration. What would this sudden discovery of wealth do to his wedding plans? she wondered.

He was still watching her expectantly, and she abruptly abandoned that line of thought. "It is highly irregular to allow a child to attend an assembly, my lord, but in the circumstances I think no one would take it amiss, providing Christabel stay a very short time only. But I—I fear I have nothing suitable to wear," she finished lamely, realizing how inappropriate it would be for she herself to appear at this particular event.

"Wear something of Amity's," suggested the earl. "You are much the same size as she was. Do say you'll come!" His eyes held a boyish appeal that she could not possibly resist.

"Very well," she said, for she could hardly refuse. "But only for a little while...." Surely no harm could come of a brief appearance as Christabel's nanny. She would tell him the truth tomorrow. No later than tomorrow.

FREDERICA WAITED until she heard a steady hum of voices below before descending to the ballroom. She hoped that with so many people in attendance, she might manage to slip in with Christabel and sit in some inconspicuous corner while the earl introduced the child about. Then she and her charge could retire to the nursery again before anyone noticed her.

The dress she wore was one of Amity's plainest, though still much finer than any she had brought along in her role of nanny. It was with some regret that she had resisted one of the more elaborate gowns, firmly telling herself that Miss Cherrystone would never be comfortable in such a dress. Clad in a simple blue poplin, she felt that she looked as she should: a prim nanny dressed up in her Sunday best to mix with her betters. Stifling a chuckle at the thought, she stooped to straighten the bow on Christabel's dress and take her firmly by the hand before entering the ballroom by a side door.

There, she stopped short. How on earth had Lord Seabrooke managed to gather so many people on such short notice? The large room was by no means filled to capacity, but it appeared to Frederica's inexperienced eyes that half of the ton must be present. As they moved farther into the room, she realized that there were, in fact, probably no more than forty or fifty people in attendance, all talking animatedly. Christabel chattered excitedly to her, but Frederica scarcely heard her as she scanned the room in search of the earl.

Since the afternoon, she had been wondering how the news of his unexpected wealth would affect his marriage plans. He patently had no need to marry an heiress now. Would he adhere to the betrothal? And did she want him to? Several hours of reflection had not been sufficient to provide her with answers.

Smiling cordially at various guests, all unknown to her, as she attempted to answer Christabel's rapid-fire questions, Frederica moved through the throng around the buffet into the relatively uncrowded centre of the room. Before she could catch her breath, they were accosted by the earl, who was smiling with delight.

"Miss Cherrystone! I was beginning to fear you meant to hole up in the nursery for the duration. Let me introduce you about. You remember Sir Thomas?" He gestured towards her brother, who had just come up.

"Of course," she replied, refusing to meet Thomas's eye. She knew that he must be wondering how much further she meant to take this charade. That she also knew his speculation was justified did nothing to restore her composure. "How pleasant to see you again, Sir Thomas," she murmured.

If Lord Seabrooke noticed her discomfiture, he gave no sign. "And my niece, Christabel," he said, taking the little girl's hand. She smiled shyly up at Sir Thomas, forcing him to withdraw his gaze from his sister to smile back at the engaging child.

"Ah, let me present to you Lord Garvey, Miss Cherrystone, and his wife, Lady Elizabeth," said the earl, before Frederica could gather her thoughts.

She turned to see a handsome, fair-haired man, younger than the earl, and a sprightly brunette lady quite evidently in the family way. She warmed to them both as they cheerfully acknowledged the introduction, with no hint of surprise in their manner at being presented to a mere nanny.

Lady Elizabeth gushed warmly over Christabel and then whisked her away to introduce her around the room herself. When she returned a short time later, Frederica almost regretfully suggested to the earl that it was time she took her charge up to bed.

"Nonsense," he said cheerfully. "Mrs. Abbott can take her up." He gestured to a passing footman, who hurried off to find the housekeeper. "I'd like you to stay and enjoy yourself."

"Oh, but—" Already, Frederica had realized the risk she was running of meeting someone here who might recognize her later. That would not do at all!

"Please, Miss Cherrystone, I insist." He held her eyes with his own for a moment and, again, she could not disappoint him.

"Very well," she said. "But only for a little while."

After half an hour of spirited conversation, and a glass of champagne that had been pressed on her by Lord Seabrooke, Frederica actually found herself beginning to enjoy the evening. As more introductions were made, she noticed that few of those present seemed to conform to Miss Milliken's description of Society's "high sticklers," in spite of their wealth of titles. She wondered whether Milly had exaggerated, or whether Lord Seabrooke merely tended to befriend the less formal members of the ton. She rather suspected the latter, from what she knew of the earl.

Gavin, meanwhile, was not enjoying himself nearly so much as he strove to appear. His thoughts kept returning to his conversation with Mr. Culpepper late that afternoon and to his own subsequent decision. When he had learned just how extensive a fortune his uncle, because of his investments, had actually left him, his first inclination had been to put an end to this betrothal that felt so wrong. Christabel—and he—could now live perfectly adequately, even luxuriously, without any dependence on Miss Chesterton's money.

Almost at once, however, he realized how selfish, how unfair, even how dishonourable such thoughts were. How could he, in conscience, refuse to marry the girl now? He had been willing enough to give her the consequence of his name when he had stood to benefit from the match. It would be reprehensible of him to attempt to cry off now that she might similarly benefit. What had at first appeared as an answer to a prayer now placed him under even stricter obligation. Before, he might have justified breaking the engagement with the honourable motive of sparing his fiancée a financially disadvantageous alliance. Now he had no such recourse.

Watching Cherry as she talked easily with his friends, he felt as though a part of him were dying. At that moment, Lord William, the Duke of Brenthaven's third son and a mad rapscallion, even for Gavin's set, raised his glass and voice.

"Here, here! Quiet, everyone! I'd like to propose a toast!" Tall and extremely thin, Lord William swayed like a reed in testament to the excellence of the champagne. Gavin watched him with some misgiving.

"To our esteemed host and his chosen bride. Gavin, if Miss Chesterton is half as pretty as she is rich, you should be a very happy man. And if she ain't, well, you'll be able to afford to take your pleasures elsewhere!" He accompanied his words with a broad wink.

An uncomfortable silence followed the toast, the majority of the guests recalling, as Lord William apparently did not, that the brother of the lady in question was present. After a moment, Lord Garvey stepped forward, prodded by his wife, and shoved Lord William unceremoniously aside.

"I will echo the first line of that toast," he said. "To Gavin and his bride—may they enjoy a long and happy marriage!"

To this toast, everyone felt perfectly justified in drinking, and the awkward moment was smoothed over. Lord William, belatedly realizing his mistake, attempted to stammer an apology to Lord Seabrooke and the glowering Sir Thomas, but the others began to talk and laugh as before.

Frederica, however, scarcely heard Lord Garvey's amendment. She stood rooted to the spot, scarlet with embarrassment and shame. Embarrassment that such a thing should be said of her, in front of all these people whose opinion she now valued, and shame at her own stupidity. For it all made sense to her now.

Why should Lord Seabrooke resist a loveless match when he could still have his pick of mistresses? Miss Sheehan's face swam dazzlingly before her. There was no reason for him to seek a release from the betrothal even now when he no longer needed the money. He need not even feel guilty that he must use his wife's money to pay for his paramours. Doubtless that would be a relief to a man so upstanding, so *honourable*—the word echoed in her mind with biting sarcasm—as Lord Seabrooke. She despised herself for her naïvety.

The occasional tenderness she had imagined in the earl's eyes when he spoke to her she saw now only as further evidence of his willingness to disregard any marriage vows he might make. Was she perhaps slated to take Miss Sheehan's place? That was not at all what she wanted . . . was it?

Shaken by the thought, Frederica suddenly knew that she needed to be alone to sort out her painful, conflicting feelings. Backing toward the door with a brittle smile on her face, she slipped out of the ballroom and hurried up the stairs. She had just reached the second landing when she heard footsteps following. Turning, she was startled to see Lord Seabrooke mounting the stairs behind her.

"You left rather precipitously, Cherry," he said as he closed the distance between them, his face concerned. "I hope you are not feeling unwell."

"I—I am fine, my lord," she managed to say, though she trembled at his nearness. "I am merely unaccustomed to champagne, to the late hour and to so many people." All of which was quite true, though it had little to do with her distress.

"I'm sorry, Cherry," said the earl with every appearance of sincerity. "I hadn't thought of that, I confess. I merely wished you to enjoy yourself—as you richly deserve!"

His smile affected Frederica as it had always done, in spite of her attempts to harden her heart towards him. To her disgust, she felt the corners of her own mouth curving upwards in response.

"That reminds me," said the earl before she could think of anything to say. "There is something else you deserve and that I very much want you to have." He pulled a roll of notes from the pocket of his evening clothes. "I promised you a bonus, if you recall. Here it is." He handed the money to her.

Frederica took it automatically, then glanced down. He had given her fifty pounds! "My lord, please, I cannot—" she began, attempting to give it back.

"I insist," he interrupted firmly, closing his hand about hers, the money still in her fist. "In truth, this is a mere pittance considering all that you have done for me, and for Christabel. I wish I could give you far more." His blue eyes glittered with warmth, and something more than warmth, as they locked with hers.

Suddenly, Frederica found it difficult to breathe. She was very much aware of his hand on hers, of the warmth and strength of his long fingers. Desperately, not knowing what she meant to say, she parted her lips to speak.

Without warning, the earl tightened his grip on her hand, drawing her to him. His other arm went around her and he lowered his head to hers, blocking with his lips whatever words she might have summoned. Frederica clung to him, reveling once again in the hot, spicy taste of his mouth, the masculine firmness of his body against hers. Unsuspected longings sprang up, frightening in their intensity.

Probing deeper with his tongue, the earl ran his hands down her shoulders, caressing her through the thin silk of the dress. Frederica felt that she was drowning in him, but had no wish to save herself. Shamelessly, she moulded her body to his. His hands grew more insistent, touching the bare flesh at her throat, the soft upper curve of her breast.

She knew she should protest, but his touch excited her beyond reason, beyond caring. Her will would not answer to her conscience. Instead, she threw back her head as he rained kisses down the length of her throat, following the path of his hands.

With one hand, he fumbled with the buttons at her back, while the other continued to caress, sliding inside the suddenly loosened neckline of her gown. One thumb grazed the tip of her breast as the nipple rose to greet his touch.

With a muffled cry of dismay, Frederica suddenly pulled away as the enormity of what they were doing penetrated her frenzied brain. After only the briefest attempt to restrain her, Lord Seabrooke released her, his expression startled.

"Cherry, I—"

"No, my lord, don't!" She cut him off in a high, shaky voice. "I—I'll bid you good-night." She took refuge in trite, familiar words. "Pray enjoy the remainder of your evening. It was most kind in you to invite me." Still clutching the fifty pounds, which she had completely forgotten, Frederica turned and ran up the stairs without a backward glance.

Gavin did not try to stop her. He was too overcome by the incredible surge of passion that had swept over him during that moment of madness. He knew now, without doubt, that his feelings for Cherry went far beyond mere friendship. And he knew that they were reciprocated, if only in small measure. Certainly he had not imagined her response!

He should follow her he knew, to apologize for his conduct, but he was afraid to. Afraid that if he followed her to her room, he would say things, do things, that would be impossible to retract. No, better to wait for morning, when both of them would have had time to think. With one last, wistful glance at the empty staircase, he reluctantly descended to the ballroom and a celebration that now seemed more hollow than ever.

FREDERICA WAS STILL shaking when she reached her room. How could she have allowed that to happen? How could he? Unclenching her fingers, she suddenly became aware of the money that she held, and she grew hot all over.

So that was it! Unlikely as it seemed, especially given her drab disguise, that must be it. She was slated to become his next mistress, conveniently placed in his own house to carry out their intrigues under his unsuspecting bride's nose! For a moment she was nearly blinded by anger that he would callously intend to betray her so. Then, almost immediately, she was suffused by shame that he would think her willing to participate in such a betrayal.

Abruptly, she recalled Milly's words: "If you are not careful, you will end up being jealous of yourself." Was that it? Was she jealous? After a moment's thought, she had to admit that she was. Jealous as Miss Cherrystone that he would go ahead with this marriage for money; and jealous as Miss Chesterton that he would pursue an affair with Christabel's nanny while he was betrothed to her. The situation was patently absurd, but she could find no humour in it. Not now.

She remembered again those few delicious moments in his arms. She knew that she had shamelessly revealed her feelings to him, had allowed him liberties that amply justified his assumptions. And she still tingled at the memory of her response to the touch of his lips, his hands, upon her. How was she to face him in the morning?

She couldn't. Now that her body had betrayed her a second time, she dared not stay. Nor was she bold enough to go through with her intended confession. No, she would leave the house now, tonight, get away from his influence, and then make new plans. Spurred by the thought, she began to pack.

It took her no time at all to bestow her few belongings in the small trunk she had brought. Changing out of the dress she had worn to the party, she again donned the plain grey gown she had arrived in—was it only two weeks ago?

Pulling out pen and paper, she wrote a brief note accounting for her departure, one that anyone might read, though she knew that Lord Seabrooke would divine her real reason. Not until a tear fell onto the sheet before her and smudged her signature did she realize that she was crying. The fifty pounds she left in the top drawer of the dressing-table as repudiation of his offer.

Tiptoeing into the nursery, Frederica gazed down at Christabel in her little bed, serene in sleep, and envied her her unsullied innocence. The thought of leaving her tore at her heart. Leaning down, she softly kissed the child's velvet cheek, fervently hoping that the earl might somehow make her understand why she had to leave.

Tears streaming down her face, Frederica left the nursery, closing the door silently behind her. She picked up her trunk and stole softly down the back staircase and out of Seabrooke House, into the night.

CHAPTER FOURTEEN

IN SPITE OF his late night, Gavin awoke early, feeling remarkably refreshed. For a moment he could not understand his pervading sense of well-being, and then he remembered the passionate kiss he had shared with Cherry. He had a vague memory of dreams, pleasant dreams, that had centred upon her, as well.

In that moment, as he lay smiling up at the ceiling, his plans for the future crystallized. He could never be happy with anyone but Cherry as his wife. Somehow he must persuade Miss Chesterton to call off the betrothal. He would call on Sir Thomas that very morning to discover just how set on the match she really was. Then, once that matter was taken care of, he could lay his heart before Cherry.

His mind clearer than it had been in weeks, Gavin fairly leapt out of bed, ready to execute his plans. He had just finished shaving when Metzger made his appearance, obviously startled to find the earl already awake and alert.

"Good morning, m'lord. Would you like me to... Oh, I see you've already shaved. Mrs. Abbott has asked to speak to you at once. I told her you wouldn't likely be down for an hour or more, but—"

"Thank you, Metzger, I'll be down directly. You may tell her to wait in the library," replied the earl cheerily. His valet helped him to shrug into his coat, then went to report to the housekeeper while Gavin tied his cravat. Even the complicated *en cascade* gave him no trouble today.

Humming merrily, he descended to the library to ascertain what Mrs. Abbott wanted. Doubtless something pertaining to last night's gathering. At the sight of the housekeeper's distraught face, however, he stopped humming.

"You wished to speak with me, Abby?" he asked at once, his manner slightly more subdued. Mrs. Abbott was not easily upset, he knew; only something very much out of the ordinary could account for it.

"Oh, my lord! I don't know what to do, and that's the truth. She's gone!" His normally sedate housekeeper was actually wringing her hands.

"Gone?" he echoed. "Who is gone? Christabel?" Sudden alarm surged through him.

"No, my lord. 'Tis Miss Cherrystone. Miss Christabel discovered her gone this morning and came to find Lucy. She left in the night, seemingly, and took all her things with her! All she left behind was this."

Gavin snatched the proffered sheet of paper from her hand, his alarm increasing to dread. He read through the brief, polite note, in which Miss Cherrystone apologized for leaving without notice and hoped that he would convey her affection and best wishes to Christabel.

In short, it told him nothing. He knew at once, though, why she had gone. What must she have thought when he had all but ravished her, then let her go without a word of apology? She knew that he was engaged to be married. With her elevated principles, it must have seemed to her that the only thing she could honourably do was to leave before they could do anything they might regret. But damn her principles! He wanted—needed—her back!

Belatedly, he became aware of Mrs. Abbott still regarding him anxiously. "Doubtless she has gone to her friend's house here in London," he said reassuringly. "I shall find her."

"Pray do, my lord. Miss Christabel is most upset, and will be even more so if she learns Miss Cherrystone don't mean to return. The child needs her—and so do you, if you'll pardon my saying so." Mrs. Abbott actually patted him on the shoulder as she rose to go. She had obviously not missed the anguish in Gavin's eyes.

"I believe you are right," he said with a rueful smile at the unwitting echo of his own thoughts. "Do reassure Christabel while I make enquiries."

FINDING MISS CHERRYSTONE did not prove so simple a matter as Gavin had predicted. By late that afternoon, he was growing increasingly frustrated—and anxious, as well.

He had known, of course, that many of Cherry's references had been false. As their friendship deepened, he had more than once thought that she was on the verge of telling him the truth about her background, but she had never done so. Now he discovered that not one of her impressive list of referrals could help him to locate her. In fact, none of the people he queried discreetly through Jeffries had so much as heard of a Miss Cherrystone. It was as though she had materialized on his doorstep out of thin air, and had so returned.

When Jeffries delivered a polite negative to his fifth enquiry, he swore in exasperation. "Blast it, she must have worked somewhere before coming here! What of her friend, the one she visited on her half days?''

Jeffries was unable to help him, so the earl went out to the mews himself to speak to his coachmen. With mounting frustration, he discovered that Cherry had never availed herself of their services, always hailing a hackney when she left the house.

''I don't suppose anyone happened to notice which one?'' he asked without much hope. They had not.

Fighting a sense of despair, he returned to the house. After a moment's thought, he mounted the steps to the fourth floor. Perhaps he could find something in her room to give him a clue.

It seemed that Mrs. Abbott had unfortunately been quite correct. The only thing he saw was the borrowed dress Cherry had worn to the party the previous night. At the sight of it, laid neatly across the narrow bed, Gavin's precarious control began to crumble. He felt closer to crying than he had at any time in his adult life.

A slight noise from behind him served to pull him from his painful reverie. He turned to see Christabel standing in the doorway to the nursery, regarding him with big, serious eyes.

''She's not coming back, is she, Uncle Gavin?'' she asked softly. One crystal tear trickled down her cheek.

Swiftly, Gavin knelt to take her in his arms. ''I don't know, Sunshine,'' he said huskily. ''I hope she will.'' They clung together for a few moments, comforting each other for their mutual loss.

Finally Christabel stirred and looked up at him. ''Perhaps Cherry was really a good fairy who came to help us. Perhaps she thought her work was done here, and she went away to help someone else.''

"Perhaps," he replied with a twisted smile. In truth, it seemed as plausible an explanation as any he had been able to devise.

Gavin remained with Christabel until her bedtime, playing with the pet mice—Cherry had left these for Christabel, she'd said in her note, along with the peacock—and sitting at the table with her while she ate her dinner. The child seemed to draw some measure of comfort from his presence, as he had to admit, he did from hers.

Once the child was asleep, he methodically examined Cherry's room. Nothing remained in the clothespress, he quickly discovered, turning his attention to the dressing-table. Pulling open the top drawer, he saw the roll of pound notes he had given her last night and froze. Suddenly he understood. What must she have thought when he kissed her, caressed her so intimately, only moments after pressing the money into her hand?

As he realized what conclusion she must have drawn, Gavin closed his eyes in horror and self-loathing. How could he have been so stupid? And now she was gone, hiding somewhere in the vastness of London, without a farthing, so far as he knew. She had not even received her regular wages as yet.

He opened the other drawers, but found nothing else. Finally he gave it up and went down to the dining-room, where his own dinner awaited him. He had no appetite, but picked at the excellent meal before him, unwilling to go into the library, where so many memories of Cherry lurked. Instead, he had his customary port brought to him at the table.

Swirling the wine in his glass, he stared into the ruby depths and reviewed what he had accomplished that day. Surely he could have done more, perhaps question the other servants in the homes in which Cherry had claimed previous employment.

At that thought, he sat up straighter. Of course! What a dolt he had been! Here he sat, one of the military's best agents for ferreting out information, sending formally worded notes about Town through his footman. If ever his skills and experience in intelligence could prove useful, surely it was now!

Instantly translating thought into motion, he rose from the table and called for his coat and gloves. Major Alexander was ready for action again.

UPON LEAVING Seabrooke House, Frederica had at once attempted to hail a hackney. Depositing her awkward trunk beside her on the curb, she had looked up and down Upper Brook Street without seeing one. Some short distance away, a group of young men were laughing and singing together, their arms linked. Frederica had never before been on the streets of London so late at night, and she wondered nervously if her decision to leave, which had seemed so inarguable when she made it, had in fact been wise.

The rowdy group was heading slowly in her direction, hampered by occasional stumbles and lurches. Just as she was considering the advisability of swallowing her pride and returning to the house, she saw a hackney coming up the street from the opposite direction. Praying that it might be empty, she waved her hand.

Mercifully, the hackney stopped, and the driver was obliging enough to help her with the trunk. "Where to, miss?" he asked cheerily, once it was safely stowed.

Frederica gave him the direction of the house where Thomas had taken lodgings, and they moved on just as the band of young bucks reached the spot where she had been standing.

Sir Thomas was just returning from Seabrooke's assembly as the hackney drew up in front of his lodgings.

"Thomas!" cried Frederica out of the window, causing him to stop and stare.

"Freddie? What the devil—"

"I'll explain in a moment. Do help me with this trunk, there's a dear," she said briskly, her spirits reviving now that she no longer had to fear being locked out, which disturbing thought had occurred to her during the short drive.

A few minutes later, the jarvey had been paid and Frederica and her trunk were safely ensconced in Thomas's rooms on the third floor.

"Now, suppose you tell me what necessitated your coming here in the dead of night rather than waiting till tomorrow, when I shall have the keys to the house on Audley Square. I shan't have to call Seabrooke out, shall I?" Thomas's tone was teasing, but Frederica could see the wariness in his eyes.

"Of course not!" she exclaimed quickly, horrified at the idea of Thomas and Lord Seabrooke fighting. Now that it came to it, she found that she had no desire to tell her brother the truth—especially after his last remark! "It was just that during the...the assembly tonight, I realized how odd my position was and decided to leave before any more damage was done. Suppose any of the people I met there should recognize me when I enter Society?"

To her relief, Thomas seemed to consider that explanation plausible enough. "Well, I suppose you can stay here the night. I was going to go out again—stop into a new club down on Jermyn Street—but I suppose that can wait. You take the bedroom and I shall camp out here on the sofa."

Frederica gave him a quick hug. "Thank you, Thomas. And this way, I shall be here to take care of moving into the house you have let. I am most eager to see it!" she lied, determinedly keeping her tone cheerful. "Tomorrow I'll send a note round to Milly, and she can join us at Audley Square. She has promised to play chaperone for a few weeks."

"I shall leave all that in your hands, Freddie. You will know what to do better than I." He gave her a crooked but genuine smile and went to find an extra blanket for the sofa.

The next morning, Frederica rose somewhat later than she was accustomed to doing, and discovered her brother still soundly asleep. Rather than wake him, she went back to her room to prepare herself for the day ahead.

A small mirror hung on the wall above the washstand, and she glanced into it, automatically straightening the brown wig, which, out of habit and fatigue, she had worn to bed. Then she stopped.

Miss Cherrystone no longer existed, she suddenly realized. From this moment on, she must again be Miss Frederica Chesterton of Maple Hill. She pulled off the wig and regarded it wistfully for a moment before carefully placing it in her trunk, along with the glasses. She was going to miss "Cherry." She had a sudden vision of Lord Seabrooke's face, and Christabel's, and her eyes misted over. Fiercely, she shook her head. That phase of her life was done with!

To distract herself, Frederica scrubbed her face nearly raw, removing all traces of her false freckles, and brushed out her copper curls. Her own things, along with her abigail and a few other servants from Maple Hill, would arrive at Audley Square later that day. Until then, she would have to wear one of the plain gowns from the trunk.

While she dressed, Frederica began the thinking and planning she had been too tired—and too unsettled—to do the night before. Now, in the sober light of day, she could consider things a bit more dispassionately.

The recollection of Lord Seabrooke's caresses still had the power to make her giddy, she discovered. Firmly, she pushed away the memory and attempted to concentrate instead on possible motives for his actions. The one she wished with all her heart to believe was that he cared for her. That he considered her a friend, she had not doubted—until last night. But was it more than that?

Recalling the liberties that he had taken, that she had allowed him to take, she decided it seemed far more likely that he wished her to be his mistress. Did gentlemen love their mistresses? She did not think they did, as a rule, though she was woefully ignorant about the subject. But neither did they necessarily love their wives. It occurred to her that she would far rather be loved as a mistress than merely tolerated as a wife. Her cheeks growing pink at the scandalous thought, she tried again to think rationally.

Had his actions been indicative of love? She had fallen head over ears for the earl in the brief time she'd known him, but she couldn't quite believe that he had done likewise for the plain Miss Cherrystone. Perhaps the kiss had merely been an expression of gratitude, an attempt to convince her that he really wished her to accept the bonus he'd given her, and which she'd tried to refuse. It might well have been her own shameless response that allowed it to become so much more. That seemed a depressingly reasonable explanation.

And what now? Now that she knew what it was to love, could she endure being married to a man who had her heart in his keeping while his own was free? Could she hide her feelings for him, pretending only friendship, while he pursued his own pleasures elsewhere? No, she could not!

Her dress fastened, Frederica turned to regard herself critically in the mirror. The scrubbing had left a rosy glow in her cheeks, and she realized with a start, seeing her undisguised face as though for the first time, that she was really quite pretty. Perhaps the bran-faced, bespectacled Miss Cherrystone had not been able to win the earl's heart, but as Miss Chesterton, properly gowned and coiffed, in fashionable surroundings, she might have a chance. Certainly it was worth a try!

By the time Thomas stirred, it was past eleven. Frederica had tidied the entire apartment and packed his belongings in preparation for the move to Audley Square. She was more than ready to be on her way, and to set her plans into motion.

The majority of the day was spent settling in to their temporary home. All Frederica's management skills were brought to bear as she hired servants, wrote letters and dealt with the details attendant on moving into the house for the remainder of the Little Season.

Miss Milliken came at once upon receiving Frederica's message and was installed in the room next to hers.

As they worked side by side for the rest of the day, setting the house in order, the former governess sent many a questioning look Frederica's way. Their conversation was limited, however, to the number of housemaids they would require or the rearrangement of the furniture. Not until they finally found themselves alone for a belated cup of tea in the late afternoon did they give voice to the topic occupying both their thoughts.

"Well, my dear, does all this mean that you finally managed to tell Lord Seabrooke the truth?" Miss Milliken asked, after waiting a few moments in vain for Frederica to broach the subject.

"Not...not precisely, Milly," Frederica admitted, refusing to meet her companion's eye. "But I felt it was high time I left Seabrooke House."

Miss Milliken knowingly regarded the girl before her. "You have come to feel more than mere friendship for Lord Seabrooke, have you not?"

Frederica nodded dumbly.

"Would you like to tell me about it?" Miss Milliken prodded gently.

Looking up to see the warm concern on her old friend's face, Frederica suddenly felt her eyes fill with tears. "Oh, Milly! I've done the most foolish thing! I've fallen in love with him and I don't know whether he cares for me or not." With a profound sense of relief, she poured out the whole story to Miss Milliken, along with her suspicions and fears. The only details she omitted were those moments of passion, which were still too private, too precious, to share.

"So when he gave me the fifty pounds and...and looked at me so, I didn't know what to think. I was afraid if I stayed longer I would betray my feelings to him. Oh, how *can* I marry him now, if he does not care for me? That is why I have decided to storm his heart...as myself." She continued to outline her plans for the next two weeks.

Miss Milliken listened to the entire recital in silence. When Frederica was done, she asked, "Then you plan to keep your identity as Miss Cherrystone a secret from him?"

"For the present, at least," replied Frederica. "If I disguise my voice somewhat, and am careful to keep my eyes downcast, I believe I can carry it off. If...if my plan works, if we can reach an understanding, then it should be safe enough to tell him the truth."

"Deceit may be a valuable strategy in war, Frederica," said Miss Milliken quietly, "but I cannot think that it has any place in love. There, honesty is surely the best policy."

"Once I am confident of his love, I fully intend to be honest," Frederica assured her. "But until then, are not all policies allowed in war and love?"

CHAPTER FIFTEEN

THE FOLLOWING MORNING, Frederica, with a still-dubious Miss Milliken in tow, began the next stage of her plan. They visited the best modistes and milliners, ordering the very latest styles in gowns, bonnets and accessories. Frederica was now dressed in one of her newest gowns from Maple Hill, but it was still sadly countrified by Town standards and did not project the image she intended to cultivate.

She also arranged to have one of the most exclusive coiffeuses in Town cut her hair, and she hired another woman to keep it styled. She had been taught to dance in the course of her education, but she nevertheless engaged a dancing master for two or three lessons to perfect her steps, especially in the newer waltz and quadrille.

In the afternoon, they repaired to Audley Square to make plans for her come-out ball at the end of the following week. During the morning's shopping, Frederica had made the acquaintance of several ladies, both married and unmarried, who were highly placed in the ton and who had promised her invitations to a few upcoming soirées. More than one of the older ones had recognized Miss Milliken, greeting her as a long-lost bosom-bow. Frederica had wondered at it, but her friend had not volunteered an explanation.

"Tomorrow we must call on those ladies who desired to further their acquaintance with you," Miss Milliken said after they had surveyed the ballroom the house afforded, noticeably smaller than that at Seabrooke House. "There you will doubtless meet others, and within days, if you take, you will be inundated with far more invitations than you will have time to accept. Your own should go out no later than Friday, by the by."

"Will that not be very short notice?" asked Frederica in surprise. "The ball will then be only a week away."

"That cannot be helped. You will need that much time to make the necessary connections to ensure that it is not overlooked entirely. I did take the precaution of mentioning the date to Lady Humphries while you were being fitted at Madame Jeannine's. She was able to assure me that it should not conflict with anything *too* important, such as her own ball this Thursday. That is likely to be one of the most significant gatherings of the Little Season. To do this thing properly, you really should have been in Town—officially—at least two weeks earlier." It quite obviously irritated Miss Milliken to be forced to rush what should have been a most organized and careful campaign.

Frederica wisely changed the topic, saying, "Where did you meet Lady Humphries, Milly? She appeared to know you quite well."

For a moment she did not think that Miss Milliken would answer, but after a brief hesitation, she said, "Lady Humphries and I attended the same ladies' seminary when she was still Miss Bryant. That is also where I met Mrs. Thackeray and Lady Wimberly. By then, however, I was a teacher there."

"What seminary was that?" asked Frederica, gratified to gain some insight into her friend's mysterious past. When Miss Milliken told her, she gasped, for it was easily the most famous—and expensive—boarding school in England, patronized by the highest families of the ton.

"But...but how did your parents—" she tentatively began.

Miss Milliken cut her off. "An uncle was kind enough to pay my tuition. Now, how soon did the modiste say that your new habit would be ready?"

Frederica saw that any further discussion of Miss Milliken's history would not be tolerated. Accepting the mild rebuke at her curiosity, she obediently allowed the conversation to move to the gowns she had ordered that morning.

BEFORE NOON the next day, Frederica and Miss Milliken sallied forth again, this time to make the requisite morning calls. Their first stop was at the home of Lady Humphries, who was very highly placed and who, Miss Milliken told Frederica as they alighted from the carriage, could be of immense help in establishing her if the woman were so inclined. During the brief drive, Miss Milliken had been at her most pedantic, reminding her onetime charge of various rules of etiquette, apparently determined that Frederica do credit to her teaching. Frederica was equally determined not to disappoint her former governess.

They were shown into a spacious, elegantly appointed salon, where Lady Humphries was already entertaining one or two other callers. At their entrance, she immediately rose to greet them.

"My dear Charlotte!" she gushed, coming forward to embrace Miss Milliken. "I am so glad you are come. Pray, let me introduce you and Miss Chesterton to Mrs. Phipps and her daughter."

They passed a pleasant quarter hour there, though Frederica found Miss Phipps a trifle flighty for her taste. Still, the girl was friendly enough, insisting that Frederica call her Gwendolyn and relating all the more important scandals that had occurred since the start of the Little Season.

"For these stories are bound to come up elsewhere, and you would not wish anyone to think you ignorant of the latest on-dits, I assure you, my dear Frederica!" she said with a titter.

Frederica smiled but said little, striving to listen to the conversation among the three older ladies whenever Miss Phipps's tongue paused, in hopes of learning something of more consequence. Still, what Gwendolyn told her was enough to make her realize how easily her reputation could be shattered were her masquerade as Miss Cherrystone ever to become known. None of the "scandals" related even remotely compared to the magnitude of that social breach.

After taking leave of Lady Humphries, they called at the home of Mrs. Thackeray, another of Miss Milliken's former acquaintances. Here Frederica got her first taste of the backbiting that could occur under the guise of polite conversation, for it soon became obvious that Miss Sylvia Thackeray had entertained hopes of becoming Lady Seabrooke herself and had been much disappointed by the announcement that had appeared in the papers a few days previously.

"So you are to be Lord Seabrooke's new countess," she said with a sugary smile when they were introduced. "How daunting a prospect it must seem to one so newly arrived in Town! You have lived your whole life in the country, have you not?" Her thickly lashed brown eyes raked over Frederica critically as she spoke. "Town life is different, I assure you. And what responsibilities you will face in that exalted position! Pray do not hesitate to come to me for advice when you should need it," she added, implying that she was far more qualified to handle the duties of a countess than a rustic like Frederica could possibly be.

"Thank you, Miss Thackeray," responded Frederica, matching the other girl's syrupy sweetness, though her green eyes glittered dangerously. "But I shall endeavour to muddle along as best I can. With my dear Lord Seabrooke's help, I cannot think I shall find any task too arduous." Her own smile was limpid.

Sylvia sniffed. "Then we must hope he is not too often from your side," she said with an answering spark of malice.

Frederica knew that the girl referred to the earl's reputation as a rake and was just about to deliver a scathing set-down when she caught Miss Milliken's slight frown and subsided. Milly had warned her that this sort of thing was bound to happen, given her fiancé's popularity with the ladies. She had not expected it quite so soon, however.

Shortly after this exchange, Frederica and Miss Milliken took their leave.

"I am proud of the way you handled Miss Thackeray, Frederica," said Miss Milliken as they walked the short distance to their next call. "I am amazed that Bertha could have raised such an ill-mannered girl. Pray do not let her words trouble you."

Frederica agreed that she would not, though she could not help but wonder what sort of attacks would be levelled at her as she became more visible in Society. There were pits and snares that she had not even considered, it would seem.

They had not been above five minutes in Lady Wimberly's drawing-room when two other ladies came to call, making Frederica aware of yet another tangle awaiting her. One of the newcomers was Lady Elizabeth, Lord Garvey's wife, with whom, as Miss Cherrystone, she had conversed at some length only three nights before!

Frederica kept her voice low as she replied to the introductions and, as she had planned to do when she encountered Lord Seabrooke, she avoided meeting Lady Elizabeth's eyes. Instead, she looked at her companion, the Duchess of Ravenham, a lovely woman with unusually long, golden-brown hair.

"Miss Chesterton is but recently arrived in Town, your grace," their hostess told the young duchess. "You may have seen her name in the society pages, for it is she who has finally caught our elusive Lord Seabrooke. Their betrothal was announced a few days ago, much to the disappointment of half of the young ladies in London—and their mamas!" She chuckled with amusement. Frederica had already discovered that Lady Wimberly had no daughters of her own.

The Duchess of Ravenham, was all that was friendly, and Frederica warmed to her as she and Lady Elizabeth shared stories of their first Season. She was delighted to discover that she and the duchess, who insisted that Frederica call her Brie, had in common a love for animals.

"Though now I find that most of my time is taken up with a different sort of animal, with which I had no previous experience," said the duchess, laughing.

"Brie! Are you calling my nephew an animal?" asked Lady Elizabeth in mock indignation. In an aside to Frederica she said, "If she were not so determined to flout convention by taking on the bulk of little Derek's care herself, she would have no cause for complaint, you know. But already I begin to think I may follow her example!" She folded her gloved hands against her swollen figure complacently.

Frederica thoroughly agreed with that particular bending of Society's rules. Certainly she would prefer to have a large part in the care of any children she might have! That thought led inevitably to Lord Seabrooke, and the last time she had seen him.

To distract herself, she turned to Lady Elizabeth and said, "I collect that you and the duchess are sisters-in-law?" She had become so comfortable in their company that her earlier fears were quite forgotten and she looked directly at the other woman as she spoke.

"Oh, yes! I forgot that you could not have known, being so newly arrived in Town. Brie is married to my brother, Dexter, the Duke of Ravenham." She paused, a slight frown creasing her white brow. "But are you absolutely certain that we have not met before, Miss Chesterton? There is something exceedingly familiar about you."

In sudden panic, Frederica averted her eyes. "Perhaps you have met my own brother, Sir Thomas," she said quickly. "Some people have remarked on a certain resemblance between us."

Lady Elizabeth's brow cleared. "Oh, yes, I have—at Lord Seabrooke's. That must be it."

Frederica began to breathe normally again, but allowed the others to dominate the conversation for the remainder of the visit. She could not help but hope that a time might come when she could reveal everything to these two ladies, with whom she would like to become friends. Somehow, she thought they just might understand.

GAVIN STIFLED AN OATH. Three days of diligent sleuthing had brought him no closer to discovering Miss Cherrystone's whereabouts—or origins.

"Are you certain that no one mentioned driving such a person from Upper Brooke Street, perhaps to the outskirts of Town?"

The hackney driver shook his head again. "Not as I c'n recall, m'lord. Course, there's nothing much to remember, meaning no offence. Brown hair 'n' spectacles ain't so very remarkable."

"No, I suppose not." The earl thought hard. What detail could he offer that one of the drivers might have noticed and told his cronies about? While *he* found Miss Cherrystone far out of the ordinary, there was no denying that her looks bordered on commonplace. Her special qualities were not likely to be perceived by a jarvey taking her for a short drive.

"...young buck with a bright green wig!" the driver was saying. "Now that's somethin' I'll recall to me dying day. Or Old Joe—he was tellin' me about some woman insisted on bringing along a peacock! I ask you!" The man chortled, wiping one grimy hand across his mouth. "By gum, if it'd been me—"

Gavin looked up in sudden excitement. Of course! "Where can I find this Old Joe?" he demanded, interrupting the jarvey's reminiscences about his queerer fares.

He seemed unperturbed, doubtless owing to the gold coin the earl had already given him. "At this time of day? I don't rightly know. You might try the business district—Threadneedle 'n' such. A dark blue hackney, he drives, used to belong to Lord Linley, or so he says."

He trailed off, for the eccentric nobleman was already walking quickly back to his own carriage. "Thank ye, m'lord!" he called, flipping his easily earned guinea in the air. "If'n ye need any more questions answered, just come to Chalkie!"

Gavin lost no time in finding the man referred to as Old Joe. As Chalkie had suggested, he was plying the business district at that hour and was more than willing to allow Lord Seabrooke to transfer from his crested carriage into the battered old hackney he drove.

"Chalkie tells me you drove a lady with a caged peacock recently," said Gavin, climbing up to sit on the box beside the grizzled driver.

The old man frowned, but before he could open his mouth, Gavin pulled another guinea from his pocket and the frown was magically smoothed away. "That I did, m'lord," he said promptly.

"Take me to the house where you picked her up and this is yours," said Gavin.

"Aye, guv—I mean, m'lord. Right away!" Old Joe whipped up his pair of nags and headed out of town at a spanking pace.

"This be the place, m'lord," he said a short time later, drawing up before a respectable-looking cottage.

Gavin surveyed it critically. No one seemed to be about. "Are you certain?" he asked.

"Aye, that I am. I won't soon forget that ride, with that gaudy heathen bird squawkin' the whole way!"

"Very well, then, here you are." Gavin flipped him the coin. "You may go." His own carriage, which had followed them, drew up behind. With a touch of his hat, Old Joe clattered off down the street, doubtless wishing more eccentrics with well-lined pockets would come his way.

Gavin strode up the flagged walk and rapped on the cottage door. Finally he was getting somewhere! A moment later he knocked again, more loudly this time. If no one was at home, he decided, he would damned well camp on the doorstep until someone returned. This was by far the most solid lead he had had.

He was just raising his hand to pound on the door again when it opened, revealing a bent, grey-haired man. "Yes? Oh, it's you!" he exclaimed in apparent delight.

Gavin was taken aback. He was almost certain he had never seen the man before. "Good afternoon, sir," he said politely. "I've come to ask—"

"Well, don't stand there on the step, Kenneth, come inside!" said the man, opening the door wide. "I told Charlotte you'd be coming back today."

The earl blinked. "Charlotte? Sir, I fear you have mistaken me for someone else. My name is not Kenneth."

At that moment, a maidservant hurried out of one of the rooms and placed one hand on the elderly man's arm. "Come back to your dinner, won't you, sir?" she said cajolingly before turning to the earl. "I don't know what you wanted, sir, but you'll likely want to leave a message for Miss Charlotte. The master's mind tends to wander a bit."

"Miss Charlotte?" asked Gavin, his hopes soaring. Surely that would be Cherry! "Is she not here?"

"No, sir, nor expected back for some weeks. Would you care to leave a message?"

"Weeks?" Gavin's spirits plummeted from their sudden peak. She was not here. But surely he could discover where she had gone! First, though, he must be certain. "Would she have green eyes, by chance, and freckles? About twenty years of age?"

"Oh, no, sir. Miss Charlotte would be much older. She has brown eyes, and I never noticed no freckles."

"My Charlotte is the very image of her mother," the old man affirmed, nodding emphatically. "She'll grow up just as lovely, I'll be bound."

Gavin smiled uncertainly at the master of the house, who obviously spent much of his time in the distant past. "And is there no one here who fits that description? A servant, perhaps?"

The woman shook her head. "I'm the only one here now, besides the master and his man-of-all-work. I do the cooking and housekeeping, while John does the heavy work and gardening. Would you like to speak with him?"

Gavin shook his head. "You must excuse me for disturbing you. I seem to have mistaken the address."

During the drive back to Seabrooke House, he pondered the recent interview. If Old Joe had not been mistaken, Cherry had come from that house; it seemed wildly improbable that two young women had transported a peacock in a hackney within the past week! But where was she now?

Back in his library, he tried to think what he should do next. Should he go back to that house, perhaps disguised as a delivery man? Idly, he picked up the stack of correspondence that had accumulated in his absence.

Among the various invitations and letters of business, he found a note from Sir Thomas. He opened it absently, still mulling over what his next step should be. He had to scan the note twice before its import registered.

"Confound it!" he exploded, crushing the missive in his fist.

Miss Frederica Chesterton was in Town.

CHAPTER SIXTEEN

LADY HUMPHRIES'S ball would be Frederica's first formal function in Society, the first occasion for her to see and be seen by the most influential members of the ton, but that was not the real cause of the anxiety she felt. Of far more importance to her than the impression she might make on the Prince Regent, who was expected to attend, was the fact that this evening would likely mark her first meeting with Lord Seabrooke as Miss Chesterton.

At her suggestion, Thomas had yesterday sent word to the earl of her presence in Town. She had both hoped and feared that he might call on her during the course of the day, but he had not. Now she was rather relieved; she felt she had a much better chance of carrying off her deception in a ballroom than she would in private conversation. If all went as she hoped, she would not have to fool him for long.

Her nerves aflutter, she critically examined herself one last time in the cheval glass. Her red-gold curls were piled high on her head, with tiny white flowers woven through them. The white gown she wore was sprigged with green, flattering both her hair and her eyes—not that she planned to let Lord Seabrooke get a good look at her eyes, of course! Still, it was vastly comforting to know that she looked her best. She practised flirting with her green-and-white silk fan, pleased with the effect. Surely Lord Seabrooke would not be able to resist her as she was now!

"Frederica, are you ready? It will not do to arrive after the Prince Regent himself," Miss Milliken informed her, coming to the door of her boudoir.

"Yes, Milly. Let us go." Holding her head high to conceal the tremor she felt, Frederica descended the broad staircase to where her brother waited.

"BLAST IT, Metzger, not like that!" Lord Seabrooke rounded on his hapless valet, ruining yet another neckcloth. "Here, I shall tie it myself." As he deftly knotted a fresh square of the snowy linen into a flawless Orientale, he glanced at the man at his side. "I'm sorry, Metzger, it isn't your fault. I am in the devil's own temper tonight."

Metzger nodded silently. Such outbursts and apologies had become increasingly frequent since Miss Cherrystone had left, but his master's mood was more dangerous tonight than he had yet seen it. Doubtless it had to do with the fact that within the hour he would be meeting his fiancée for the first time. It was a pity, that, but none of Metzger's business, he well knew.

A short time later, Gavin stood at the top of the staircase leading into Lady Humphries's magnificent ballroom. Surveying the glittering throng before him, he wondered dispiritedly whether Miss Chesterton had yet arrived.

He should have called on her earlier in the day, he knew, but had not been able to bring himself to do so. What possible reason could he give her for wishing now, at this late date, to dissolve their betrothal? Was he to say that he loved another, even though that other had seemingly fallen off the face of the earth? It sounded lame even to himself. Taking a deep breath, as he had often seen Cherry do in times of stress, he vowed to at least give Miss Chesterton a chance. It was by no means her fault that they were in this absurd situation.

Gavin had just begun to mingle with the crowd when he spotted Sir Thomas bowing over Lady Humphries's hand. With him at the head of the stairs stood a handsome lady who must be Miss Chesterton's companion, and a vision in white crowned with copper. Miss Chesterton's eyes were demurely downcast as she made her way into the throng on her brother's arm, but her complexion appeared flawless and her hair fairly glowed above the whiteness of her shoulders. His bride-to-be was no antidote, that much was certain!

Still, Gavin had to force himself to step forward to greet the Chesterton party. No matter how lovely she might be, she was not Cherry.

"I am most gratified to finally make your acquaintance," he said when Sir Thomas had performed the introductions. Even to his own ears the formal greeting sounded stiff almost to the point of rudeness. Hastily, he attempted to soften it. "Perhaps you would be so gracious as to grant me the first dance?"

"Certainly, my lord," she replied in a voice so low that it was almost a whisper. With a sinking heart, Gavin realized that Miss Chesterton must be extremely shy of him. What a contrast to Cherry's plucky outspokenness! And he felt no particular inclination to draw her out.

"Pray allow me to present you to my acquaintance," he said, offering her his arm. It would look deuced odd, he realized, if he were to abandon her the moment she arrived.

She placed delicate fingers on his arm and obediently accompanied him into the crowd. Gavin duly introduced her to several of his friends, as well as to such exalted persons as a patroness of Almack's and two of the royal dukes. The Prince was not yet in attendance. Seabrooke was surprised to discover that Miss Chesterton had already met some of those present; he would not have thought she had the gumption even to go out of the house on her own. Perhaps her companion had insisted upon it.

Though for the most part Gavin kept his gaze averted from the lovely creature at his side, an occasional glance was necessary as he made the introductions. Each time he looked her way, however, she quickly averted her eyes. This was going to be more difficult than he had thought. How could he possibly jilt such a shrinking violet without appearing the greatest brute in the realm? Even Cherry—especially Cherry!—would never forgive him.

It was with relief that Gavin heard the orchestra begin playing a minuet. After the set he could reasonably leave Miss Chesterton on her own for a while. They took their places and moved through the dance. With some surprise, Gavin noticed that his partner's steps were flawless, and none of her apparent nervousness showed as she dipped and curtsied as the dance demanded. How had she learned to dance so well, immured in the country?

As the dance brought them back together, she flashed him a brief look. Gavin started involuntarily at the emerald green of her eyes before she again shaded them with her long lashes. A sudden memory of Cherry assailed him, and he had to steel himself inwardly. He had been imagining her likeness everywhere he looked for days. Now he was even attempting to find a resemblance in the unlikely person of Miss Chesterton! Absurd!

When the dance ended, he delivered her back to her chaperone and made his bows, promising to return for the supper dance before decamping.

Frederica watched him go with mingled regret and relief. This was going to be far harder than she had expected. How could she charm the man when she couldn't even look at him or speak clearly? But she dared not. She had not missed the sudden flicker in his expression when she had accidentally allowed him to see her eyes. Had she held his gaze as the minuet actually called for, she would already be undone. She must not let him catch her looking at him again.

For, indeed with surreptitious glances she had been drinking in the sight of him, so precious after these few days of separation. And she had been secretly appalled at the changes she could perceive. Somehow, in less than a week, he had lost his sparkle, his vitality, that zest for living that had always drawn her to him. He also appeared to have lost weight. Had he been ill, she wondered? Her senses sharpened by love, Frederica noticed what no one else would have: that Lord Seabrooke appeared far from happy.

As she danced a quadrille with Mr. Gershom, she puzzled over the realization. She had known all along, of course, that Lord Seabrooke had been less than enthusiastic about his betrothal to her, but that hardly seemed cause enough to account for the dramatic difference in him tonight. He had seemed resigned, if not content, when they last spoke of his forthcoming nuptials. Tonight he almost looked liked a man whose heart had been broken.

From that thought, another occurred to her so suddenly that she almost missed her step. Could it be possible that he really had fallen in love with her as Miss Cherrystone—that her leaving had hurt him so badly? The idea filled her with guilt even as it gratified her. She could not wish on him the sort of pain she herself had been subject to at their parting, even though it might indicate that his feelings were all she had hoped.

But what was she to do now? How was she to know for certain? As the quadrille ended and a country dance began, she scarcely noticed the change of partners, so full was her mind with the dilemma before her.

"My dear, what a success you are!" exclaimed Miss Milliken more than two hours later, when Frederica had consented to sit out a dance with her brother so that he might procure some lemonade for her. "Lady Humphries tells me that your card was full before the dancing had even begun."

"Yes, I suppose it was," said Frederica absently, scarcely noticing the distinguished-looking gentleman at her companion's side. "But Lord Seabrooke asked only for two dances. As we are betrothed, he could quite properly have requested three, or even more." She had been acutely aware of the earl—and his many partners—throughout the evening.

"Can you blame him, Frederica?" asked Miss Milliken gently. "From what you tell me, this match was scarcely more to his taste than it was—originally—to your own."

Startled at her friend's outspokenness, Frederica glanced quickly at the stranger standing nearby.

"Oh, let me present to you Mr. Westlake," said Miss Milliken, with a slow smile that caused Frederica to sharpen her gaze. "He and I met years ago, and have been renewing our acquaintance after a long hiatus."

"Yes, I well remember Charlotte when she made her debut back in '95," said Mr. Westlake, smiling at his Miss Milliken in a way that Frederica would almost have called besotted. "She is the only female I have ever known who truly appreciates military history, a particular passion of mine. Indeed, she was the brightest diamond of the Season that year, but disappeared before I, or any of my many rivals, could place her in the setting she deserved. I am delighted that she is come back to us at last."

To Frederica's astonishment, Miss Milliken blushed at this recital. "Your memory is quite obviously addled by time, Charles. I was nothing out of the ordinary, then or now."

As Mr. Westlake began to protest, Sir Thomas arrived with lemonade, interrupting the fascinating exchange.

"Egad!" he exclaimed, mopping his brow with a handkerchief. "No doubt Lady Humphries is in alt because of the crush, but I'd as lief there were fewer people here. You'd best drink up, Freddie, for the set is nearly over."

Frederica obeyed, suddenly recalling that the next dance, the one heralding supper, was promised to Lord Seabrooke. Perhaps she should have asked for champagne, she thought belatedly. It might have given her courage.

Even as she chided herself for such faintheartedness, Lord Seabrooke materialized to bow over her hand. To her dismay, the orchestra struck up a waltz. The earl clasped her lightly, almost impersonally, and swept her into the dance.

Involuntarily, Frederica glanced up at him, recalling the last time she had been in his arms. It had been so different then! There had been fire between them; now there was only this strained politeness. Surely there must be some way she could get through the shield he had raised against her!

"My brother tells me you fought on the Peninsula, my lord," she said coquettishly, fluttering her lashes in the manner she had seen more than one of his other partners doing. She kept her voice light and breathless, quite unlike her normal tone. "How very brave of you, to be sure!" As she had noticed before, his dancing was superb, not at all affected by his limp.

"Merely my patriotic duty, Miss Chesterton," he said coolly, looking over her head after only the briefest glance at her face.

She tried another sally. "I vow, I would have been frightened to death, being shot at by the French!" Again she fluttered her lashes, but to no avail. This time he did not even look at her, only acknowledging her comment with a tight, impersonal smile.

So it appeared that Lord Seabrooke was impervious to flattery and flirtation. After a moment's thought, Frederica realized that he had probably been subjected to so much of it that it no longer affected him. Which was just as well, for that sort of thing was not really in her style anyway. Perhaps a different tactic would be more effective.

"What thought you of Wellington's campaign, my lord?" she asked a moment later. Between Thomas's passion for the recent battles and Miss Milliken's influence, she was certain she could hold her own in a conversation about warfare. However, she was not to be given the chance.

"It worked," the earl said briefly, refusing to elaborate.

Frederica resisted an urge to shake the man. How on earth could she hope to captivate him—or even to learn anything of his state of mind—if he would not talk to her? She stole another glance at him and was distressed by the unhappiness she detected in his face. Could she be the cause of it? The idea unsettled her enough that she attempted no more conversation before he led her in to supper.

For his part, Gavin was trying desperately to dispel the fantasy that it was Cherry he held in his arms instead of Miss Chesterton. Her feeble attempts at flirtation, while revealing that she was not quite so shy as he had feared, only served to confirm that she was in no way like the girl he missed so much. Only her eyes reminded him of Cherry. He wondered if green eyes would always torment him so—and whether he could endure being reminded of Cherry every time he looked in Miss Chesterton's face. Surely, there must be an honourable way out of this farce of a betrothal!

Perhaps if he were to speak to her brother? The betrothal had been contracted in lieu of payment of that wretched wager. Suppose he agreed to release Sir Thomas from his debt, to repay the marriage settlement? It might be worth a try.

Supper was a lively meal, but only because Gavin and Miss Chesterton were joined by Lord Garvey and his wife, and the Duke and Duchess of Ravenham, whom Gavin knew only slightly. The latter were an engaging pair, he found, and rather unconventional, in spite of the duke's reputation as a high stickler. It appeared that marriage had mellowed him somewhat.

"And you actually helped to whelp the puppies yourself?" Miss Chesterton was asking the duchess in disbelief. "Were you successful?"

"Oh, yes, I had done it countless times before, with my father. Once that first big pup—who was breach, to compound things—was out of the way, the others came along right enough. Odd as it sounds, that was rather a special time for Dexter and myself," responded the duchess gaily.

While the conversation flowed around him, Gavin found himself studying his fiancée. There was certainly no denying that Miss Chesterton was a beauty. Her bright curls, flawless complexion and those lovely eyes, so like Cherry's, were a bewitching combination. He felt a stirring of response and berated himself for his disloyalty. How could he be drawn to this girl when the one he loved was lost, perhaps even in danger somewhere?

Ruthlessly, he suppressed the attraction he felt. He knew well enough that beauty alone could never hold his interest over the lifetime a marriage entailed. Had not all his mistresses been beautiful? They, too, had kindled his desire—but never his love. Other men might be willing to risk their future happiness for a pretty face, but not he.

Other men? Of course! Now that he saw what a beauty Miss Chesterton was, why should he feel guilty at the thought of dissolving their betrothal? There must be dozens of men, many far wealthier than he, who would be more than willing to take his place.

In order to confirm that hypothesis, Gavin spent the remainder of the evening watching Miss Chesterton and her admirers closely. And yes, there were many, many admirers. Among them was Lord Auldin, a marquess who was reputed to be one of the wealthiest men in England. He appeared completely besotted by her, staring down into her eyes as they danced and holding her far closer than even the waltz demanded. The set after that she was partnered by Mr. Tremont, not so wealthy as Auldin, but still far richer than Gavin himself. He also appeared thoroughly smitten by her charms.

No, she was not likely to suffer from a termination of their betrothal, particularly if he could convince her to cry off, thus sparing her any embarrassment. Sternly ignoring an errant thought that perhaps being married to her would not be such a bad thing after all, Gavin decided that he would call on Sir Thomas tomorrow to discuss it.

CHAPTER SEVENTEEN

HER SCHEME had been a dismal failure, Frederica had to admit, as she reviewed the events of the ball upon awakening late the next morning. Lord Seabrooke had been perfectly polite, but she had detected far more admiration in Lord Auldin—in half of the other gentlemen there, in fact—than in her fiancé. And she was no closer than she had been at the outset to discovering what his feelings towards Miss Cherrystone had been!

On descending a short time later, she discovered that no fewer than eight bouquets had been delivered for her already that morning. Eagerly, she examined the cards, but not one was from Lord Seabrooke. She knew she should be gratified that she had "taken" so well, but that one omission overshadowed the ample evidence of devotion from her other admirers.

Dejectedly, Frederica made her way into the breakfast-room, where she found Miss Milliken, in oppressively high spirits, eating sausages and eggs.

"Good morning, Frederica! Is it not a lovely day? What a pity that Town hours require us to sleep through half the morning." With a cheery smile, and looking somehow far younger than she had the day before, she speared another bite of sausage.

"You must have enjoyed yourself far more than I did last night, Milly." Frederica attempted to keep the gloominess she felt out of her voice, having no wish to dampen her friend's good humour.

"Indeed, I had a far better time than I expected. Who would have thought that I should see Mr. Westlake there? I had nearly forgotten the marvellous weeks we spent in each other's company during my brief Season, but he quickly brought it all back to me." She sighed happily, causing Frederica to regard her in amazement. "He is to take me driving shortly, and specifically suggested that you come along—as *my* chaperone. Is he not absurd? As if a woman of my years needed one."

Observing Milly's giddy mood, Frederica was not so sure she did not. "I shall be delighted to come along, Milly," she said, attempting to summon a teasing manner. "I wish to learn more of this Mr. Westlake, to discover whether he is worthy of you."

Miss Milliken actually tittered at this, causing Frederica to stare at her in wonder. Was this her staid governess? She would not have thought such a transformation possible. Spending an hour or two in her company might be the very thing for her own depressed spirits.

BEING WITH two undeclared lovers who patently delighted in each other's presence was far from uplifting, Frederica found. Instead, it only served to heighten her awareness of what was lacking from her own life. To distract herself from such thoughts, she set about observing Mr. Westlake, as she had jokingly told Milly she would.

Mr. Westlake was every inch the gentleman, and though unfailingly attentive to Miss Milliken, he remembered to include Frederica in their conversation.

He owned a very comfortable estate in the north, she discovered, and had apparently never married, though he was now well past forty.

"After Charlotte disappeared, no other could take her place," he said, with such a fond look at her friend that Frederica felt distinctly *de trop*. "My parents wished me to marry, of course, but as my younger brother had already done so, the requisite heir was virtually assured. Having known true love, how could I settle for less?"

Miss Milliken snorted, though the smile never left her face. "What devotion you now profess, Charles! If you were so in love, why did you not come after me?"

"I tried. Honestly, I did." He half turned, catching Frederica's eye with a rueful smile. "Though perhaps not as hard as I might have. When a fortnight of enquiries did not produce her direction, I confess I gave it up. I was still young then, remember. It was not until later that I fully realized what I had lost. I'll not allow you to give me the slip again, my dear." Now he spoke solely to Miss Milliken. "I want your father's direction, as well as that of every other person connected with you, before you leave Town this time." Recalling his manners, he turned back to Frederica. "Perhaps you can help me in that, Miss Chesterton."

Frederica absently agreed, her thoughts on his earlier words. Had Lord Seabrooke attempted to follow Miss Cherrystone? Would he also have given up by now? Looking at Miss Milliken and Mr. Westlake in their present happiness, she was struck by the wasted years behind them—twenty years of happiness they might have enjoyed had Mr. Westlake been successful in finding Milly when first she left London. Would she herself one day look back in similar regret? Would the earl?

She determined that it must not be. Rather than face such a bleak future, she would risk his anger, even her own embarrassment, by revealing the charade she had employed. If nothing else, he might at least allow her to visit Christabel again. She missed the child far more than she had expected to.

LESS THAN half an hour after Frederica and Miss Milliken left with Mr. Westlake, Lord Seabrooke came to call at Audley Square.

"Is Sir Thomas in?" he enquired of the footman who answered the door. On being answered in the affirmative, he handed the man his card and said firmly, "Be so kind as to tell him that I wish to speak to him at his earliest convenience."

Gavin was shown into the parlour. While waiting for Sir Thomas to appear, he carefully thought over what he intended to say. He hoped to conclude this interview quickly so that he might have the afternoon in which to further investigate Cherry's whereabouts. His one clue was that cottage where the girl with a peacock had supposedly been taken up. He had not thought to ask Old Joe what her destination had been. If it indeed proved to be Seabrooke House, he would know for certain that it must have been Cherry, and he would never rest till he discovered where she had gone. And if it had not... He refused to think further on that possibility, which led only to despair.

"Good morning, Seabrooke," said Sir Thomas, entering the parlour. "I am told Frederica has just gone out, but she should be back within an hour or so. She always was an early riser."

"No matter," said the earl. "It was you I wished to speak with." Gavin waited until Sir Thomas had made himself comfortable before launching into his speech.

"As you know, my betrothal to your sister occurred as a result of a gaming debt on your part. At the time, I was badly in need of funds, and this seemed my best chance of obtaining them. However, that does not excuse what I did. I essentially forced you to engage your sister to me, without making the slightest effort to discover her feelings on the matter."

"Forced?" echoed Thomas. "No, I say, that's coming it a bit strong—" He stopped as Lord Seabrooke held up his hand.

"Please, hear me out. Whatever your thoughts were at the time, the fact remains that neither one of us consulted Miss Chesterton's wishes. Having met her, I realize now that she could no doubt have her choice of any number of highly placed, wealthy gentlemen for a husband. It seems most unfair to hold her to this betrothal, which was made without her consent."

Sir Thomas appeared nonplused, but not, as Gavin had feared, angry or distressed. "But my wager...?" he stammered.

"I am willing to forgive the debt entirely, and return what you settled on your sister. I have recently come into funds that will enable me to live quite comfortably without it, and I cannot rest easy knowing what we have done." He watched Sir Thomas keenly, trying to decipher the conflicting emotions on the young man's face.

"Is your sister truly set on the match?" he asked in sudden concern. "If so, of course I cannot renege."

"No, no, I don't think so. In fact, she was dead set against it when I first broke the news—" said Thomas candidly "—though she seems to have come round now. Still, twelve thousand pounds..."

"A small price to pay to avert years of possible unhappiness, both for your sister and myself. And I have had use of the money for more than a month, do not forget. I'll gladly consider it a loan." He managed to summon a smile.

"What about the announcement? It's been in the papers this week and more."

"She may cry off, of course, and the public will be duly notified. It seems only fair that I be the jilted party, as she was blameless in all this."

Thomas exhaled noisily. "Well! Won't Freddie be flummoxed when I tell her! And after all her scheming—" He broke off, looking almost guilty, but brightened at once. "Very well, then, Seabrooke. It shall be as you say. I must admit, I am relieved. I would never have forgiven myself if Frederica had been unhappy. This way, it will be her own choice."

"Quite," said Gavin shortly, eager to be gone. He had little doubt that Miss Chesterton would avail herself of the opportunity he had given her, especially now that he knew what her feelings had been at first. She had not seemed comfortable in his company last night, and now he could understand why. Looking about him, he noticed for the first time the veritable garden of bouquets that had been delivered, and thought, with a pang that surprised him, that she would have no trouble finding someone to replace him.

"I'll be off, then. Be so kind as to send me word of when the retraction will appear in the papers." He rose, nodded briefly and departed, trying to convince himself that he had done the only honourable thing.

"WON'T YOU come in, Mr. Westlake?" asked Frederica when the carriage pulled up in Audley Square. She spoke automatically, her thoughts still busily engaged with how she might best arrange to speak privately with Lord Seabrooke.

Mr. Westlake agreed at once, obviously loath to part from Miss Milliken just yet. The three of them repaired to the parlour, where Mr. Westlake politely exclaimed over the flower arrangements.

"Lovely. Quite lovely. And your success is very much to Charlotte's credit, if I may say so." He turned another lingering look on Miss Milliken.

On impulse, Frederica said, "Would you do us the honour of dining with us this evening, Mr. Westlake? Our cook is excellent, as Milly can assure you."

When he allowed that he would very much like to join them, she said, "I shall just nip downstairs to tell Cook." As quickly as their courtship seemed to be progressing, Frederica felt that a moment alone might be all that was needed to bring it to a satisfactory conclusion. Leaving the parlour door slightly ajar to preserve the proprieties, she walked unhurriedly down to the kitchens.

An extra place at dinner presented no problems, and she was soon done with her consultation with the cook. She was considering what other duty she might perform to give Milly and Mr. Westlake more time to themselves when Thomas came out of the breakfast-room, having just finished his own belated meal.

"Freddie! The very person I wanted to see. You will never believe what occurred while you were out!"

Mindful of the occupants of the parlour, Frederica steered her brother back into the breakfast-room. "What is it, Thomas?" she asked. "You look inordinately pleased with yourself. Have you placed a bet on a winning horse?''

"Even better," he said, beaming. "Seabrooke has cancelled my debt to him!''

"Cancelled it?" For a moment, Frederica's mind refused to function. "What do you mean, Thomas? I thought my betrothal to him had discharged it. Did you not say that twelve thousand pounds of my inheritance had gone to pay it?''

Thomas regarded her patiently. "That's just it. He has offered to repay the amount in full. You no longer have to marry him, Freddie!''

Frederica felt as though the world were crumbling around her. "He...he has broken off our betrothal?''

"Well, not precisely. He left that for you to do, since he could not cry off in honour. But you are now perfectly free to do so! Is it not a superb jest? When I think of the lengths you went to to free yourself from him, and now he releases us from the obligation as easily as that!" He snapped his fingers. "I vow, I laughed for ten minutes together after he left.''

Frederica knew her face must have gone rather white, for Thomas abruptly sobered somewhat. "Are you not relieved?" he asked uncertainly. "Now you can accept whoever you wish. I thought you would be as diverted by this news as I was.''

"Oh! I—I am," she said, trying to keep her voice steady. "Did...did he say why he decided to do this?" A faint glimmer of hope buoyed her. Perhaps, just perhaps...

"He said it wasn't fair to you. That you could obviously have your pick of suitors, and so forth. Does it matter?''

Frederica's shoulders slumped. "I suppose not," she said dully.

Thomas regarded her doubtfully. "I say, are you all right, Freddie?"

"Of course, Thomas." In fact, she felt numb all over. "This is just what I had hoped for, is it not?"

"I had thought so. At any rate, you may now do as you like. Of course, there is still the matter of your living under his roof for two weeks, but as no one discovered it, I don't suppose it really signifies. He did ask that we let him know before announcing in the papers that the betrothal is at an end. All you need do is write him a note crying off... if... if you like, that is." He was still watching her with some concern.

Frederica forced herself to smile. "How very simple," she said lightly. "I suppose I should do so at once."

"That's settled, then," said Thomas with a satisfied nod. For once, Frederica was grateful that her brother was not more observant, or he surely would have noticed how she was shaking. "I'm off to Boodle's. I shall see you at dinner." With a cheery wave, he tramped out of the house, whistling a merry tune.

For a full three minutes after he had gone, Frederica remained standing by the breakfast-room table, staring sightlessly across its littered surface. Lord Seabrooke had released her from their betrothal. He had no desire whatsoever to marry her. The room lost focus as her eyes blurred with tears.

Abruptly, she remembered Milly and Mr. Westlake in the parlour. She had been gone nearly fifteen minutes by now—she would have to rejoin them. Woodenly placing one foot in front of the other, she traversed the hallway, which seemed to stretch out endlessly before her. At the doorway, she took three deep breaths and forced a stiff smile to her lips. Pushing open the door, she paused, startled to find Milly alone.

"Here you are at last!" cried Miss Milliken at her entrance. "Charles had business to tend to before this evening, and I suggested that he leave now so that I could tell you my news alone. Oh, Frederica, I am the happiest woman alive! Charles has asked me to be his wife!"

Milly's glowing face gave evidence of her joy, and Frederica hastily thrust her own troubles to the back of her mind. Not for anything would she spoil this moment for her friend. "I can't say that I am surprised, Milly, but I can most sincerely say that I am happy for you. The two of you seem made for each other."

"Yes, I feel that way also," agreed Miss Milliken. "And he insists that we must have my father to live with us, so I need not worry on *that* account." For the first time, she looked closely at Frederica. "But you are distressed about something, my dear. You are nearly pale as a ghost! Here, come sit down and tell me what has happened."

Abruptly, she was once again the Miss Milliken Frederica knew, governess and companion. Gratefully, Frederica sank down on the sofa beside her. "Oh, Milly, I don't know what to do! Lord Seabrooke has released me from our betrothal." In halting accents, she related her conversation with her brother. "But I don't *want* to be free of him," she concluded with a sob. "And now I shall never know if he truly cared about Miss Cherrystone or not."

Miss Milliken listened in silence and then said, "Frederica, I know all too well what it is to live without love. When I think of the joyous years Charles and I might have had, the children that were never born... And all because I was too proud to tell him what I felt, or even to say goodbye when I left London."

"What...what *did* happen then, Milly?" asked Frederica curiously. Somehow, she hoped that she might be able to apply Milly's situation to her own. "Why did you leave Town so suddenly?"

"It was my uncle," said Miss Milliken with a sigh. "The one who paid for my education. He also sponsored my Season in London. Then, with the Season half over, he told me that he wished to adopt me—that I was to sever all ties with my mother. He was ashamed of her, you see. Against the wishes of her family, she had run away to try her fortune on the stage. Once she met and married my father, she left the theatre, of course, but her family never forgave her for it.

"After her father—my grandfather—died, her brother offered to support my entry into Society. He never did speak or write to her, only to me, but she was willing for me to take advantage of his generous offer. My own father could never have afforded it. She had no more idea than I what my uncle's real motive was. He had no children of his own, you see, and hoped that I might marry well, as his adopted daughter, and elevate his social standing. I believe he also saw it as a way to punish my mother for what she had done so many years before."

Frederica patted Miss Milliken's hand comfortingly. "I—I had no idea, Milly. How terrible it must have been for you."

Milly smiled. "The worst part was leaving Charles, whom I believed was near to offering for me. But I could not have accepted him under the circumstances. I was determined to receive nothing more from my uncle. I went home to my parents, who were then poorer than ever, and managed to obtain a position teaching at the seminary where I had so recently been a pupil. The rest you know. I cannot regret it, for if I had not done so, I would never have come to Maple Hill as your governess." She gave the girl at her side a hug. "What I do regret is the pride that kept me from revealing all to Charles before I left. My uncle had convinced me that I would be banished outright by the Polite World if anyone were to discover what my mother had been, and that I could not bear."

Miss Milliken shook her head over the youthful folly that had led to so many unfulfilled years. "Do not allow that to happen to you, Frederica," she said suddenly, almost fiercely. "Do not allow pride to stand in the way of love."

Frederica blinked, for Milly's words echoed her own decision made during the carriage ride only an hour earlier. But that had been before Lord Seabrooke had made it so clear that he wished nothing further to do with her. Could she now risk the pain of almost certain rejection? He expected only a note from her, a polite communication freeing him from his obligation to her. He expected never to have to face her again.

Slowly, a spark of determination grew within her. No, she would not submit so tamely. Frederica gave Miss Milliken a hug and kissed her cheek before rising. "Thank you, Milly. As always, you have given me excellent advice."

She would go to him, demand an explanation for his sudden *volte-face*. If he made reference to another love, if he so much as hinted at caring for Miss Cherrystone, then she would reveal all. If he did not . . . she would free him. She loved him too much to do otherwise.

CHAPTER EIGHTEEN

GAVIN WALKED WEARILY up the steps of Seabrooke House. He had been unsuccessful in finding Old Joe, though he had spent more than two hours haunting the narrow streets of the business district. For the hundredth time, he wished he had thought before to ask the man where he had delivered the girl with the peacock, rather than blithely assuming that his search was at an end.

He still had Jeffries out combing the streets for Joe's battered blue hackney. If they did not locate it that day, he would go back to that cottage anyway, first thing in the morning, and question everyone there. Now that he was as good as free of his betrothal to Miss Chesterton, there was nothing to stop him from laying his heart at Cherry's feet—if he could only find her!

Daniels, his new butler, opened the door for him. "My lord! There is a young lady here to see you. She came alone." His tone was severely disapproving; Daniels had far higher standards than his predecessor, as Gavin had already discovered.

"A young lady?" he echoed hopefully. Could it be...? "Did she give a name?"

"Miss Frederica Chesterton, my lord. I have put her in the front parlour. If you wish, I shall inform her that you will be out for the rest of the day."

Gavin's spirits fell even lower for their brief elevation. "No, I had better see her. Thank you, Daniels."

It appeared that Miss Chesterton was not as complaisant about his solution as he had expected her to be.

Frederica looked up as he entered the parlour, and Gavin was struck once more by her beauty. Quickly, guiltily, he suppressed a vague stirring of desire. Then, for the first time, Miss Chesterton looked him directly in the eye, and he was reminded even more painfully of Cherry. Nor were the words she spoke in greeting calculated to help him forget his loss.

"Lord Seabrooke, my brother tells me you wish to dissolve our betrothal." Her voice, though still low, was clear and oddly familiar. He must have grown accustomed to it the night before. "Might I ask why?"

For a moment, Gavin thought over the excuses he had given Sir Thomas, that his suggestion had been more for her sake than his. At the same time, the real reason—Cherry—loomed larger than life in his mind's eye. He felt he could almost touch her. But how could he possibly explain that to the girl before him? No, better to use the same reasons he had expressed to her brother. Some part of his inner struggle must have shown on his face, for even as he opened his mouth to repeat them, she spoke again.

"I already know what you told my brother. However, I believe you owe me the courtesy of telling me the real reason."

Gavin closed his mouth and swallowed. Suddenly he saw Miss Chesterton as a real person, with real feelings. Somehow he had not been fully aware of that before, so wrapped up had he been in his own problems.

"Yes, I suppose you are right. I do owe you that much," he finally said. "The reasons I gave your brother were merely those that I used to assuage my own guilt over the business. None of this has been fair to you, from the very start."

She frowned at that, and moved as though to speak, but subsided as he continued.

"I don't know whether your brother has told you this, but he agreed to betroth you to me in payment of a gaming debt." She nodded composedly, though her colour noticeably deepened. "It was wrong in both of us, but that is neither here nor there. When I agreed to marry you, I thought that a marriage of convenience was all that I wanted. In fact, I fairly scorned the idea of a love match, for I did not then fully believe that love existed. Now I do."

Frederica held her breath, afraid to hope. She had trembled when she demanded the earl's true reason, knowing what she risked. Now she would be forced to accept whatever he told her, however painful it might prove.

"Perhaps your brother has mentioned that I am guardian of my four-year-old niece, Christabel," he continued. Frederica nodded again, with barely suppressed eagerness. "I engaged a nanny to care for her, a young woman of high principles and compassion. Her...her name is not important just now. Though she was only with us for a matter of weeks, in that time I came to appreciate her true worth. We became... friends."

He appeared to grope for words, his expression clouding. "In fact, I grew to love her—first, for her kindness to Christabel, and then to me, and, finally, for herself. Whether my feelings were returned I still do not know. A day or two before you came to Town, I acted rashly. While thanking her for everything she had done for...for Christabel, I was overcome by my feelings and I—I fear I may have frightened her." As he spoke, Frederica relived that precious moment. It seemed impossible to her that he could not sense her turmoil, that the strength of her feelings did not reveal her to him.

"She knew that I was engaged to be married. I had not yet sorted out what I should do, not yet fully admitted to myself that I loved her. What she must have thought . . . !"

The handsome planes of his face twisted with strong emotion, and the torment in his once-sparkling blue eyes almost made Frederica gasp. Tears pricked her own eyes as she shared in his pain.

"I let her go, thinking to explain everything in the morning, when my mind was clear. Stupid, stupid mistake! In the morning she was gone, and I have yet to find her again. But when I do—" his expression became determined "—I plan to tell her of my love, to ask her to be my wife. You must see why I cannot continue with this . . . this betrothal, as honoured as any man would be to have you as his wife. Not now that I know what love—true love—is." His eyes were pleading.

Frederica could endure no more. She loved him far too well to allow his suffering to continue—suffering of her own making! Taking a deep breath, she stood and stepped closer to him. "My lord, there is something I must confess to you as well," she began shakily.

At that moment, she heard a commotion out in the hall, through the door that the butler had left discreetly ajar, just as she had done earlier with Milly and Mr. Westlake. A child's voice, familiar and beloved, was speaking.

"She's in here, Abby! I heard her!" The door was thrust wide and Christabel burst into the room, the horrified housekeeper just behind her, glancing wildly from one of the room's occupants to the other.

"My lord, I am so sorry," Mrs Abbott began. "I don't—"

"Cherry! Cherry! Cherry!" Christabel's cries of delight drowned out her explanations. Without hesitation, the little girl flung herself forward, wrapping her arms around Frederica's legs and forcing her to sit abruptly again on the sofa. "You did come back! I knew you would!"

Gavin stared. Instead of correcting the child, or even looking surprised at the interruption, Miss Chesterton returned Christabel's hug and pulled her onto her lap. "I missed you so very much, darling," she said softly.

"Please, please promise you won't ever go away again!" Christabel snuggled up to her and tightened her clasp around Frederica's neck.

Gavin stood dumbstruck as Miss Chesterton looked up at him questioningly, her enormous green eyes—Cherry's eyes—swimming with tears. "May I promise her, my lord?" Her voice was chocked with emotion, but it also was indisputably Cherry's.

"Cherry?" he said disbelievingly. "How...when..."

Christabel rounded on him. "Don't let her leave again, Uncle Gavin! Please?"

Staring at Frederica with eyes newly opened, Gavin wondered how he could have been so blind. He had danced twice with her the night before, spent an hour with her at supper.... Though he still did not fully understand, he smiled, his first real smile in days. "I should like her to stay for always—if she is willing."

Frederica returned his smile with a tremulous one of her own. "I am perfectly willing, my lord." Her cheeks were wet, but happiness and love, pure love, shone from her eyes.

She then glanced down at Christabel, who was bouncing on her lap with delight, and said in an al-

tered tone that sounded precisely like the nanny he remembered, "Whatever do you have all over your face,
young lady?"

"Freckles," answered Christabel readily. Gavin noticed then that his niece's face was decorated with spots
and circles of brown. "I found this pencil under your
bed and gave myself freckles, just as you used to do,"
she explained matter-of-factly.

Frederica turned bright pink and Gavin exclaimed,
"You little imp! Do you mean to say that you knew all
along that Cherry's—Miss Chesterton's—freckles were
false? Why did you not say so?"

"Do not all ladies who want freckles paint them
on?" asked Christabel innocently.

Gavin was torn between a desire to shake her and to
laugh. He gave in to the latter. "The eyes of a child see
more clearly than those of a jaded old fellow like myself, it would appear. Go with Abby, then, and wash
your face, Christabel. Cherry will be here when you
return."

With a final, fierce hug, Christabel relinquished her
hold on Frederica and followed the housekeeper from
the room. As soon as they were alone, Gavin came to
sit next to Frederica.

"I still cannot credit it," he said, shaking his head.
"How did you do it? And why?"

"As you once observed, my lord, I have strong
opinions. When my brother told me of our betrothal,
I was determined to undo it, if I could. Miss Milliken
helped me to obtain the post, and to disguise myself."

"Miss Milliken—your companion? Does she perchance live in a cottage at the edge of Town?" At her
nod, he shook his head. "And I never thought to ask
for a name," he murmured. "So you came here in an
effort to escape our engagement? How so?"

"I thought that if I could spy upon you, from within your own household, I might find something to your discredit that would convince Thomas to release me from it. It seemed a perfect plan." Frederica gave him a rueful smile. "Little did I know how my feelings would change once I came to know you. I meant to prove you a scoundrel. Instead, I found you to be a man of honour, a man I could not help but love."

"Then you forgive me for what I did?" he asked seriously. "For forcing you to this betrothal, and for trifling with your affections while you were here as Christabel's nanny? For not explaining to you then what my own feelings were?"

The depth of love in his eyes made her catch her breath. "If you will forgive me for the deception I practised on you," she replied. "And for the pain I put you through as a result of my cowardice."

He chuckled. "I suppose neither of us is entirely blameless. But if love conquers all, as they say, we can put all of our past sins behind us and begin afresh."

Taking her in his arms, he kissed her lingeringly, passionately, with no hint of restraint. Frederica returned his kiss wholeheartedly, her every sense fully alive. As he probed deeper, she opened to him willingly, eagerly. This was a kiss to seal their troth, to bind them together—forever. And it was just a taste of the pleasures to come.

"Love conquers all," she murmured, when she could speak again. That was the one point of strategy Miss Milliken had forgotten to mention during all of their scheming, the most important one of all.

THREE UNFORGETTABLE HEROINES
THREE AWARD-WINNING AUTHORS

Untamed

MAVERICK HEARTS

A unique collection of historical short stories that capture the spirit of America's last frontier.

HEATHER GRAHAM POZZESSERE—over 10 million copies of her books in print worldwide
Lonesome Rider—The story of an Eastern widow and the renegade half-breed who becomes her protector.

PATRICIA POTTER—an author whose books are consistently Waldenbooks bestsellers
Against the Wind—Two people, battered by heartache, prove that love can heal all.

JOAN JOHNSTON—award-winning Western historical author with 17 books to her credit
One Simple Wish—A woman with a past discovers that dreams really do come true.

Join us for an exciting journey West with
UNTAMED
Available in July, wherever Harlequin books are sold.

MAV93

Relive the romance...
Harlequin and Silhouette
are proud to present

by Request

A program of collections of three complete novels by the most
requested authors with the most requested themes. Be sure to
look for one volume each month with three complete novels by
top name authors.

In June: **NINE MONTHS** Penny Jordan
Stella Cameron
Janice Kaiser

**Three women pregnant and alone. But a lot can
happen in nine months!**

In July: **DADDY'S** Kristin James
HOME Naomi Horton
Mary Lynn Baxter

**Daddy's Home... and his presence is long
overdue!**

In August: **FORGOTTEN** Barbara Kaye
PAST Pamela Browning
Nancy Martin

**Do you dare to create a future if you've forgotten
the past?**

Available at your favorite retail outlet.

HARLEQUIN Silhouette

REQ-G

Harlequin is proud to present our best authors and their best books. Always the best for your reading pleasure!

Throughout 1993, Harlequin will bring you exciting books by some of the top names in contemporary romance!

In July look for *The Ties That Bind* by  JAYNE ANN KRENTZ

Shannon wanted him seven days a week....

Dark, compelling, mysterious Garth Sheridan was no mere boy next door—even if he did rent the cottage beside Shannon Raine's.

She was intrigued by the hard-nosed exec, but for Shannon it was all or nothing. Either break the undeniable bonds between them... or tear down the barriers surrounding Garth and discover the truth.

Don't miss THE TIES THAT BIND ... wherever Harlequin books are sold.

Fifty red-blooded, white-hot, true-blue hunks from every State in the Union!

Beginning in May, look for MEN MADE IN AMERICA! Written by some of our most popular authors, these stories feature fifty of the strongest, sexiest men, each from a different state in the union!

Two titles available every other month at your favorite retail outlet.

In July, look for:

CALL IT DESTINY by Jayne Ann Krentz (Arizona)
ANOTHER KIND OF LOVE by Mary Lynn Baxter (Arkansas)

In September, look for:

DECEPTIONS by Annette Broadrick (California)
STORMWALKER by Dallas Schulze (Colorado)

You won't be able to resist MEN MADE IN AMERICA!